THEORIES OF IDEATION

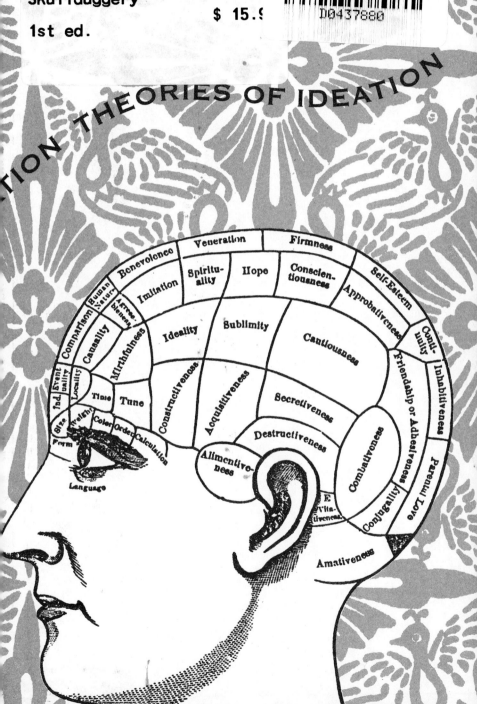

Veneration

Benevolence

Firmness

Spiritu-
ality

Hope

Conscien-
tiousness

Self-Esteem

Human Nature

Comparison

Agree-
ableness

Imitation

Approbativeness

Causality

Mirthfulness

Ideality

Sublimity

Cautiousness

Conti-
nuity

Event
uality

Locality

Constructiveness

Friendship or Adhesiveness

Inhabitiveness

Time

Tune

Acquisitiveness

Secretiveness

Size

Weight

Color

Order

Calculation

Destructiveness

Combativeness

Parental Love

Form

Alimentive-
ness

E
Vita-
tiveness

Conjugality

Language

Amativeness

SKULLDUGGERY

KATHLEEN KARR

HYPERION BOOKS FOR CHILDREN/NEW YORK

FIRST EDITION
3 5 7 9 10 8 6 4 2

Printed in the United States of America.

Library of Congress Cataloging-in-Publication Data
Karr, Kathleen
Skullduggery / Kathleen Karr.—1st ed.
p. cm.
Includes author's note.
Summary: In 1839, twelve-year-old Matthew's job as assistant
to the phrenologist Dr. Cornwall takes him up and down
the Eastern Seaboard and to Europe, as they rob graves and try
to find out who is following them and why.
ISBN 0-7868-0506-4 (trade)—ISBN 0-7868-2439-5 (lib.)
[1. Phrenology—Fiction. 2. Grave robbing—Fiction.
3. Adventure and adventurers—Fiction.] I. Title
PZ7.K149Sk 2000
[Fic]—dc21
99-39426

This is Daniel's book.

H<small>E'D NEVER TAKEN SUCH A RISK.</small>

Matthew clung to the ship's railing with both hands, ignoring the icy spray drenching him as they plunged through the rough South Atlantic. His entire being, body and soul, was focused on the mass of jagged cliffs that had just emerged from the ocean's depths after three months of nothingness.

St. Helena. The island at the end of the world. The place of ultimate exile. The Emperor Napoleon's last empire. And now they'd come to fetch Bonaparte back home. Matthew swiped at his salt-encrusted face. He blinked and the island disappeared in a swirl of mists. In a moment it reappeared, a little closer, a little harsher-looking. He had spent three months of his life, three months of the year 1840, journeying toward this strange place. What was to come would be stranger still. This was the thought that truly frightened him.

CHAPTER ONE

THE AFFAIR HAD BEGUN INNOCENTLY ENOUGH. IT HAD started nearly two years before when he was barely twelve and had never even heard the name *Napoleon*. There were a lot of famous people he'd never heard of that spring. He was too busy. Too busy trying to find a job. Too busy trying to keep his stomach filled. Too busy trying to keep a roof over his head since the cholera had taken his family—and not having much success in any of these endeavors.

It was the black border around the notice in the paper that had caught his eye:

> INTERESTED IN MEDICINE?
> DR. ABC SEEKS BRIGHT LAD.
> TRAINING AND BOARD.
> APPLY NUMBER 113, BROADWAY

Matthew was interested in medicine. He was particularly interested in finding a cure for what had robbed him of his family. He carefully rubbed the mud from his boots with the same *New York Herald* that he'd used to cover himself while huddled asleep in the alley. Next he pulled a comb from his pocket and squatted low over the nearest rain puddle. Squinting fiercely, he attacked his tangle of black curls, dipping the comb into the water to slick them down. A few dabs of moisture to his eyes and a few pulls at his trousers and jacket and his grooming was complete. Ignoring his hollow, grumbling innards, he left his shelter for Broadway and the promise of Dr. ABC.

The doctor's office was up four flights of creaking stairs. Matthew was feeling light-headed by the time he reached the top landing. He weaved over the dusty, warped flooring, scrutinizing the doors along the shadow-filled hallway until stopping finally in front of a hand-lettered sign that proclaimed: ASA B. CORNWALL, DOCTOR OF PHRENOLOGY. Underneath was a notice which dangled from a nail: DR. ABC IS IN.

"Well." Matthew poked at the card. It spun to reveal its other side. DR. ABC IS OUT. That matter resolved, he stiffened his frame and knocked. Then he knocked again. Putting his ear to the door, he heard a faint, shuffling approach. He managed to pull his head back before the door sprang open.

"What is it? Office hours aren't until eleven and it's barely eight!"

Matthew stared, his eyes almost even with those of the short, stout, disheveled man before him. This was hardly his idea of a doctor. But then, he'd never heard of any study of medicine called phrenology, either. "It's about your advertisement, sir." Matthew bobbed his head deferentially. "I've come to inquire after the job. The early bird gets the worm," he added hopefully.

The doctor smoothed his crumpled robe and opened the door wider. "Benjamin Franklin's conceit, I believe," he muttered. "An excellent reference. The archetypal man of Intellect. You may enter, young man."

Matthew crossed the threshold, then froze. Eyes widening, he took in the large room, especially the side wall completely covered by shelves crowded with plaster busts intermingled with staring, grinning, skeletal heads. "Heads!" he exclaimed. "Heads and skulls!"

"What did you expect?" growled the doctor. He waved toward the pedestal smack in the middle of the room. It also held a plaster bust, but this one was smoothly bald, with numbers painted all over its pate. "Phrenology is the scientific study of the mind through the surface of the skull, you know."

Matthew stepped backward half a pace. "But, but, I thought you were a *doctor*—"

"And the mind is not part of the body? Eh? The mind can't get sick? Answer that one, boy."

Matthew had no answer. Instead, his body took over. At least his nose did. It pointed straight toward the far corner of the room, where he could make out the form of a Franklin stove partially hidden behind a folding screen. The aroma of coffee drifted toward him, attacking all of his senses at once. When was the last time he'd drunk something warm? When the last time he'd eaten? His knees suddenly gave way, his head pitched forward, and Matthew crashed to the floor.

When his eyes opened again, Matthew found himself propped against the central pedestal inhaling
coffee fumes from a cup held before his nose.

The doctor was bending in front of him.
"Here. Drink this up while I fetch some porridge. I can't have my neighbors see me dragging
a body down four flights of stairs. They distrust
my intentions enough as it is."

Matthew grasped the steaming cup and choked
on his first gulp. It was very hot, but the liquid
jolted pleasantly through his entire body. In a
moment the cup was empty, and he was alert
again. Alert enough to accept the bowl and spoon
being offered to him. He stuffed his mouth first,
swallowed, then remembered.

"Thank you, sir."

"Humbug. Porridge is cheap enough. And
when you've consumed it, perhaps you'll have
energy sufficient to introduce yourself."

Matthew ladled the gooey mess down his throat
as fast as it would go. He wasn't even certain of its
taste until he found the bowl empty. He scraped
at it with the spoon, considered licking the sides,
then thought better of it. The oats had been
sweet. Molasses sweet.

He finally looked up at the waiting man. Only then did he notice his piercing eyes. Sharp black eyes they were, set within a plump, puffy face that sat atop a plump, puffy, rumpled body. While he was eating, the doctor's robe had been replaced with a soft velvet jacket, and his longish strands of sandy-gray hair had been carefully slicked across his bald head. Matthew stared at the head for a long moment. It was as shiny as one of the doctor's busts.

"Hurumph."

Matthew jumped off the floor. "Excuse me, sir. I am Matthew. Matthew Morrissey."

"Irish?"

Matthew pulled himself tall. "No, sir. *American.*"

The doctor hurumphed again. "Well, you already know who I am. Now we both need to know if you'll do. I need a strong lad, and a clever one."

"I'm strong, sir," Matthew declared. "When I've been fed. Big for my age, too. And I can read and write."

"How well?" the doctor barked.

"Well enough to have found your notice in the paper, sir," Matthew shot back.

"Fair enough. Fair enough." Asa B. Cornwall

paced the length and breadth of his big room, carefully weaving around several large stacks of books rising helter-skelter from the floor. Then he beckoned Matthew. "We'll have to make a study of your head, of course. Your profile, too. Phrenology never lies. After I have made my analysis, we shall have a decision."

Matthew glanced at the grinning skulls and gulped. Dr. ABC was past strange, but he had provided quite a large bowl of porridge, and there seemed to be more still bubbling atop the little stove. He walked manfully toward his destiny. Or was it his doom?

"Sit yourself here."

Dr. Cornwall dragged a heavy, stiff-backed armchair nearly to the center of the room. "We'll need the best light in the studio."

That's when Matthew noticed that the doctor's room, his *studio*, was amazingly bright. He glanced around, then up. Of course. Besides several long, narrow windows beyond the screen, the ceiling was broken with its own windows. He craned his neck back, staring at the blue sky overhead.

"You approve of my skylights?"

"I've never seen such things in a roof!"

Cornwall chuckled. "Got the idea during my European travels. All the best artists have them in their studios. It saves on candles, too. Now, settle yourself while I fetch my skull calipers."

Matthew stiffened in the chair. "Calipers?"

The doctor was already bustling back with some kind of metal instrument in his hand. "Won't harm a hair on your head, I assure you, lad. But measurements are critical to reading character from the contour of your skull."

Matthew gritted his teeth while he warily watched two prongs nearing his head, then being clamped to either temple. He shut his eyes as the doctor began humming and chattering to himself.

"We'll just have to construct a little chart." He tightened the clamp around the boy's rampant curls. "We start by taking the circumference— that's the total distance around—then make us a hypothetical line from ear to ear to distinguish the anterior from the posterior brain mass. . . . My, my—"

"What?" Matthew's eyes popped open.

"Not bad," the doctor allowed. "The outward and visible signs are promising." He unscrewed the clamp, then reset the calipers from forehead to rear. "A nicely narrow, high head. Bodes well for your moral character, lad. Can't have a criminal type in my employ."

"Um," Matthew tried, beginning to work up an interest. "What would a criminal type be?"

"A broad and low head, of course. Broad and low. Sign of the most vicious murderers. And I do like to sleep securely of a night."

Matthew squirmed. "Is this going to take much longer?"

Dr. Cornwall ceased his work to give Matthew the eye. "It's going to take as long as it takes. Don't you realize I'm giving you the benefit of my years of study? Free? Why, any one of my clients would pay a pretty penny for this analysis, my boy. A pretty penny, indeed." He set back to work again, mumbling, "Base of the brain, *c, d, c . . . a* to *a*, over *c . . .*"

"Have you got many?"

The doctor pulled away again. "Many what?"

"Clients."

"Hum, well, it's been a little slow. That's why I need an assistant, after all. To help me prove my personal theories. There hasn't been much new in the business since Gall conceived the original concept and Spurzheim developed it, you know. But when I finish up my master work, *Dr. ABC's*

ABCs of Phrenology—from the Skull Out, why, then the world will stand up and take notice. Won't it!"

"I'm certain it will have to, sir," Matthew gamely replied.

"That's the right attitude! Down with the Cautionary faculty, I say!" The doctor squinted at the tiny figures atop his calipers. "I suspect that in the final analysis, you will prove to be the Intellectual type, Matthew Morrissey, with just the correct added touch of the organs of Firmness and Combativeness. Yes, that's my initial conclusion."

"Wonderful," Matthew returned. "Does that mean I get the job?"

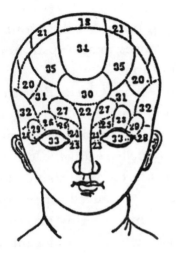

CHAPTER TWO

MATTHEW GOT THE JOB, AND IT INCLUDED ROOM AS well as board. His "room" turned out to be a cot set behind the screen in close proximity to Asa B. Cornwall's only slightly more imposing bed. His "board" consisted mainly of the porridge eternally warming atop the little stove. He didn't complain. After all, the doctor of phrenology subsisted on precisely the same fare, and *he* seemed to be thriving.

"A healthy diet, lad," Cornwall confided to him that first evening over large helpings of the stuff, "a healthy diet is key to a healthy mind."

11

Matthew resolutely cleaned out his second bowlful. "In your estimation, sir, is porridge the only healthful food?"

"Oh, my no. No, indeed. But it is the *cheapest* healthy food source. When times improve, I shall be delighted to broaden your culinary education. Share and share alike." A dreamy expression crossed his face. "Oysters . . . beefsteak . . . lamb *forestière* . . . sauced asparagus." He clattered his bowl onto the tiny table before them. "Goodness, enough of that. I suppose it's time for beginning your *general* education. I waited till evening to properly introduce you to my friends. Broad daylight is useful for scientific inquiries, but candlelight—candlelight is best for getting to really know someone."

Matthew set down his spoon. "Friends?"

The doctor picked up the candlestick. "Follow me."

Asa B. Cornwall, candle held high as in a procession, marched solemnly toward his wall of heads. He passed before them once, twice, then paused before a skull. The candlelight flickered into the eye sockets, causing curious shadows that seemed to awaken something within. Matthew almost shivered.

"Ah," the doctor sighed. "I am intimate with Joseph here." He pointed to another skull. "With Samuel, too. Intimate with all of them. They are my friends because I have studied them as deeply as anyone can study a human being, dead or alive. It's the skulls I know best. Give me a skull, and I can conjure up the very soul of a man!"

He moved the candle so that it shone on an adjoining plaster cast. "My sculptures are only second best, but better than nothing. Observe Voltaire, the most superb of French philosophers. Note the narrow, noble forehead. What thoughts passed through the brain behind that smooth façade! What I wouldn't do for the original form, the original skull, to study the brainpan's exquisite engineering—"

"*What* thoughts, sir?" Matthew interrupted.

The candle backed off a bit. "You've never heard of *Candide*?"

"I'm afraid not."

"And I don't suppose you have any French, either?"

Matthew shook his head.

Dr. Cornwall turned from his shelves to study Matthew anew—from the neck down this time. "Another week or two of porridge and I do believe you'll be up to strength."

"Up to strength for what, sir?"

"Why, for helping with the next phase of my operations. In the meantime, we shall begin your training with Voltaire. He almost single-handedly invented the Age of Reason, the great blossoming of the modern mind without which my theories would be stillborn. He was also behind a great many of the concepts incorporated into our Declaration of Independence."

His inanimate friends forgotten, the doctor scampered back behind the screen, murmuring, "Rousseau and the rest of the French, too—but then we shall have to take on Burke and the British as well. Bother!"

Matthew followed, shaking his head.

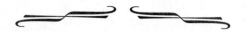

Matthew worked on completing his cleaning duties the following morning: washing porridge bowls, sweeping the floor, dusting the rows of heads. He did a little of this and a little of that as it occurred to him, since the doctor hadn't specified anything. Far from giving him orders, the man had been deeply immersed since daybreak in scribbling on the reams of paper now cluttering the tiny tabletop. Cornwall seemed to have forgotten his assistant's very presence, yet Matthew wasn't about to slack off. He was eager to do well at the job. More to the point, he was anxious not to lose it. To keep his position he was willing to do far more odious tasks than dusting skulls. Already those long days and longer nights on his own had begun to fade. He no longer had only thoughts of a happier time with his family to which to cling. Yes, a warm bed and all the oatmeal he could eat went far to make up for his new master's eccentricities.

He picked up the calipers and absently began to polish them with a soft rag. The doctor was odd, true, but he also seemed to know quite a lot. Matthew's brain was already cluttered with the surprisingly organized history of France that Dr. Cornwall had shared with him the evening before. From the monarchy to the Revolution to Napoleon, and back again. He'd found Napoleon fascinating, which pleased Dr. Cornwall enormously. And then there'd been his first French lesson.

"I'm not protesting, mind you," Matthew had protested when the lesson began, "but I'm not sure how useful French is likely to be in New York—"

"Must keep an open mind, lad. One never knows when the opportunity of travel might present itself. Then again, my patients are another consideration. An occasional foreign phrase appears to go over well with them. Since I'm not in the business of either leeching or setting bones, a bit of French or German seems to more quickly convince them that they're getting their money's worth."

Matthew thought that over. "So part of doctoring is performing?"

Dr. Cornwall beamed. "I knew my analysis of you was correct! You've quite a head on those shoulders, lad. Quite a clever head! We'll only need to add a few nuances, a little polish. It should keep us pleasantly entertained until we've gotten your muscles up to snuff."

There it was, that muscles business again. Lying on his cot that night listening to Asa B. Cornwall peacefully snore, Matthew tried to figure out why his physical strength was so important. But when the new client arrived in the morning, he was rested and more than ready to watch Dr. ABC's professional performance.

Mrs. Higginbotham had—to phrase it politely—quite a copious form. Matthew opened the door to her knock and hesitated for only an instant before bowing her in with a pleasant *"Bonjour,*

madame. Entrez, s'il vous plait." Practically his entire French vocabulary.

The goodly lady fluttered with delight before remembering the four flights of stairs. Then she rocked for a moment, breasts heaving, every inch of her flesh quivering, right down to the pudgy feet poking from her long skirt.

"La!" she exclaimed. "Such a climb!" She mopped a handkerchief around her face and neck. "But I'm quite certain the doctor will be worth it."

"*Oui, madame.*" Matthew used up the remainder of his first foreign language lesson as he bowed again.

Luckily, at that point Dr. Cornwall theatrically emerged from behind the screen. He'd torn himself from his manuscript in time to wrap a neck scarf loosely around his scruffy collar, and had even managed to button his fraying red velvet jacket over his paunch. Halfway across the room he stopped as if in wonder, and stared.

"But, madam, such a head! You will permit me to say that even from this distance, never have I seen such a bonneted head!"

The woman quivered anew, this time with pleasure. "Dr. Cornwall, I presume? I am Mrs. George Higginbotham. Actually, Elsie Higginbotham. Poor George crossed over into the great beyond just this past winter." She dabbed at her eyes with the handkerchief clutched in her grip.

The doctor moved forward, hand extended. "Allow me to offer my deepest condolences, Madam Higginbotham." He grasped her plump paw and brought it to his lips with a little smacking sound.

"*Ooh.*" The released hand flew straight to the vast vicinity of her heart. "*Ooh*, Doctor! Now I'm certain I made the right choice in coming here."

Matthew nearly gagged, then scrambled to position the chair under the best light. That done, he fetched the calipers he'd polished to a bright silver gleam. On second thought, remembering the performance elements involved, he placed the instrument upon a small tray and stood next to the doctor, ostentatiously balancing the whole thing until his employer's attention should fasten itself upon him.

Meanwhile, Dr. Cornwall was seating Mrs. Higginbotham in the armchair, solicitously removing her shawl—"So you'll be more comfortable"—and bonnet. "You'll permit? So I may examine you properly." Finally he stood back.

"Is it the three-dollar examination you'll be requiring today, madam? Or"—he coughed delicately—"the all-inclusive five-dollar examination?"

Mrs. Higginbotham sighed deeply and settled her bulk more completely. "The works! I do believe I'd like the works!"

"It would be my honor." Asa B. Cornwall caught Matthew out of the corner of his eye and turned. "My assistant has the calipers at hand." He picked them up with a smile. "But I believe we'll also be needing the *craniometer* today, Master Morrissey."

"Of course, Doctor."

While Matthew withdrew to figure out what in the world a craniometer might be, the phrenological reading proceeded.

An hour later, Matthew closed the door behind Mrs. Higginbotham while Asa B. Cornwall sank into the vacated armchair, fatigue and elation both playing over his features.

"Have you ever seen such a lymphatic type? The rounded form, the heavy countenance. A truly classic case." He shook the analysis from his head. "And did you hear her, lad? She's bringing two friends for readings tomorrow at eleven. She's treating them to the works, too!" He pulled a five-dollar coin from his pocket and flipped it exuberantly into the air. On catching it, he tossed it again, this time toward Matthew.

He captured it tidily. "It's grand news, sir!"

"Indeed," chortled the doctor. "Indeed. And my new assistant performed above and beyond the call of duty. With no rehearsal! If you can do so much with so little French—" He stopped to consider. "Imagine what a little more might accomplish! And polishing the calipers! A masterstroke!"

Matthew stroked the gold piece. "Thank you, sir. What shall I do with this?"

The doctor grinned. "With that, my lad, you will go forth into the streets of the city to find a tailor. You'll need to be measured for a suit and several shirts. Appearances are paramount in our business. Order a cravat, too. Silk. Then you will find us the biggest beefsteak in New York for our supper. Porridge is all very well in its place, but when fortune smiles, pounce upon it!"

"Indeed, sir!" Matthew grinned back. He was beginning to appreciate the good doctor's style.

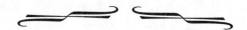

Mrs. Higginbotham returned with her two friends. Then she returned by herself for more extensive character readings. By the end of the week Matthew decided that either Mrs. Higginbotham had money to burn or she had interests in the doctor beyond his profession. The huge apple pie she lugged up four flights on her most recent visit seemed to prove the matter. As for Asa B. Cornwall, he ignored all the implications, even while gorging on the excellent pastry. Instead, he fell into a state of general elation after he and Matthew polished off the pie and sat counting their newfound wealth that Saturday afternoon.

"There's enough for the overdue rent, my boy. And enough for an overdue visit to the tailor myself. Not to mention more beefsteak."

"*More* beefsteak?" Matthew felt his stomach churn. "What about some eggs, or a nice stewing chicken for a change of pace?"

"Nonsense. Beef is what builds up the muscles! Good, red beef!"

Matthew flexed his arm. "After four nights of beef I believe my muscles are just about all built up again, sir."

"Really? Let me see." The doctor prodded and considered. "Hum. Perhaps so. Not overly fleshy, but there seems to be a certain sinewy strength in evidence. Maybe tonight we could contemplate our first excursion. It's not something we'd care to do on the Sabbath, after all. No, not at all."

"*What* isn't, sir?"

Dr. Cornwall shook his head. "Least said beforehand, the better. Here." He handed Matthew a few coins. "Stop by our landlord's room on the first floor on your way out. Give him my compliments, and the rent. Then you may procure for us a shovel and pickax of durable quality. Something for supper, too." He smiled. "You may choose."

"A shovel, sir? I don't understand—"

"You will soon enough, lad, for this very night we shall embark upon the next phase of the scientific studies necessary for the completion of my *magnum opus!*"

"What's—"

After a week of practice, the doctor already anticipated Matthew's questions. "It's Latin, my boy. For 'great work.' We'll take on that glorious language after you've a better grasp of the French. Highly useful for scientific purposes, it is."

"If you say so, sir."

"I do, indeed!"

More bewildered than ever, Matthew set off on his errands, wondering all the way. What could Dr. ABC possibly want with a shovel and pickax? He ducked into an ironmonger's shop and stopped to inspect a shovel. His father had been a brickmason. Matthew remembered how particular he'd been about his tools. Unsolicited, words poured through his mind.

You're going to be working with tools, you learn how to be one with them, son. His father's voice was as rich and strong as in life. *You don't want shabby materials. A good trowel must be balanced to a man's hand, and a good shovel balanced to the man.*

Matthew hoisted the shovel, felt its weight and balance. Unsatisfied, he moved on to another. He hadn't let his father back inside himself for a long time. Certainly not since he'd taken up with Dr. Cornwall. He hadn't had the heart for it. His father had been a proud man. Proud of his size and his strength. Proud that his eldest son was taking after him and would soon be leaving school to become his apprentice. Who'd have thought sickness could lay such a man so low? Could rob him of that strength? And his mother, so small next to his father, so pretty. And the little ones—

"Something wrong with my wares, boy? Or you just trying to see how fast they'll rust up?"

Matthew dropped the shovel to swipe at the tears running down his face. "No, sir. This one's got a nice heft. Mind if . . . mind if I try that pick?"

"Fried eggs and toast. A novel supper." Asa B. Cornwall dabbed at his lips with a napkin and shoved back his chair. He wandered over to the nearest window and peered into the night. "Ah, 'the bright day is done, and we are for the dark.' "

Matthew wiped up the last of his egg yolk with his bread and popped the crust into his mouth. Thinking about his family the way he'd been this afternoon had reminded him that he was the last of the Morrisseys. As such, he had a duty to the family not only to survive, but to make something of himself. He'd been surviving very nicely with the good doctor for almost a week, even if he had felt like a tightrope walker toeing the line most of the time. Yet certain things about the future needed discussing. He cleared his throat to work up his courage. Finally he asked the question.

"About this dark, sir. And about our excursion—"

"Yes?"

"Well, I'll need to know exactly how this fits into my job with you."

"Tut, tut. Soon enough to discuss it after the night's work. First we have to see how you react to your initiation."

The doctor sank back into his chair and Matthew's heart sank with him. All his efforts to really sort out his own role with the doctor seemed always to return to this one subject: the mysterious night excursion. He'd just have to be patient a little longer.

"And we can't begin upon the night's work," Cornwall continued, "until much later in the evening. In the meantime, why don't you fetch me that French grammar we've been working with. I've no idea whatsoever where any of my books are since you've chosen to remove them from their carefully constructed classical columns."

"But they look so much neater arranged in a row on the floor by the far wall, sir, although a few more shelves might be useful. At least your patients won't be tripping over them anymore. I've even sorted them by study: history, language, medicine, phrenology—"

"I've noticed. In one short week your organizational skills have disrupted my entire settled life. I can't find anything!"

Matthew frowned. "You should have said something sooner, sir. It's only because I've had nothing else to do—"

"You'll have plenty to do later tonight, Matthew Morrissey. I assure you of that."

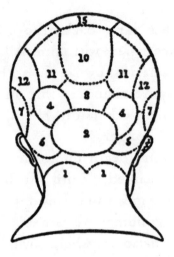

CHAPTER THREE

MATTHEW WAS NO STRANGER TO THE CITY BY NIGHT, but this particular April midnight had a chill to it that reached into the very marrow of his bones. He trembled slightly, wrapped his woolen scarf more tightly around his neck, and unwillingly slung the sack-wrapped tools onto one shoulder.

"No moon," he spoke, still loath to begin the mysterious journey. "And there's a fog settling down. It's going to be a mean one. You can barely see the brownstones just across the way."

He managed to catch Dr. Cornwall's satisfied

smile beside him under the sickly light of the street's lone lamp. "Yes. Not a living soul about. Perfect conditions for our project, lad. Absolutely perfect." The doctor's puffy face glowed a yellowish-green before he strode off along Broadway. Matthew balanced his burdens and rushed to catch up.

"You wouldn't care to explain what we're going to do on such a night, would you, sir?"

The doctor plodded forward without answer, a large satchel clutched firmly in his grip. Perhaps it was the low voices coming through the mists ahead that silenced him. Strange, disembodied voices. Matthew strained after something he couldn't quite hear, then paused at the next corner, under the next lamp, to shift his sack to the other shoulder. As he did, a form materialized from the shadows, ghostlike. A plaintive whisper reached out to him.

"Got coins in your pockets, young sir? Need a place to come in from the cold and have yourself warmed up?"

Startled, Matthew turned toward the voice. A face swam at him through the swirling mists. It was a youthful face, like his own. A girl. What could she be doing out in such a night? And without even a shawl to warm her?

"Sorry," he tried. "I've no—"

"Scat! Shoo!" Cornwall turned back to chase off the apparition. He grabbed Matthew's arm. "I thought you'd lived on the streets, Master Morrissey. You should know better than to be taken in by one of the evening crews that way."

"Taken in? By what? I wasn't on the streets that long, sir, and I was always asleep by dark when I could get warm enough," Matthew objected. He twisted to glance toward the corner and its lamp. The struggling beam of light showed only an empty circle of cobblestones, as if no one had ever been there. The loneliness of the image set off another tremor in his body. If it weren't for the doctor and his job, he could be huddling, friendless, on such a corner the way that girl was. Through his bewilderment, he finally remembered to walk again, finally remembered his current mission.

"But where are we going? And for what purpose? Shouldn't I know at last?"

The doctor poked his neck from his muffler like a turtle from its shell. He shot his head around to make certain no one else was skulking nearby, then lowered his voice. "As to where we're going, it's to Potter's Field—"

"But that—" Matthew halted in midstep. "That's a cemetery!"

"I certainly hope so, since what we're seeking is specimens for my great work."

All became clear at last. Matthew froze. "Grave robbing? You've been feeding me up to become a grave robber?"

"Well, what else did you expect?" the doctor asked testily. "How do you suppose I came by all those skulls?"

"Joseph?" Matthew's voice rose to a squeak. "And Samuel?"

"Hush!" Cornwall clamped a hand over Matthew's mouth. "You'll wake the dead! I'm not a body snatcher, for goodness sake. Not a resurrectionist. It's only the nice clean skulls I'm after, not the bodies!"

"But—"

"Can you think of a single reason why they're still needed by their original owners, boy, after the fact? By anyone but me, that is. Someone with a strong scientific interest and purpose. Someone who hopes to improve the entire world with his theories?" Cornwall tugged impatiently at Matthew's arm, but he stubbornly refused to budge.

"It's not right, sir. Surely not! It's against nature and religion!"

Asa B. Cornwall sighed. "How can it be against nature if, as I just explained, I'll be using the specimens for the betterment of nature? And as for religion, what could the Creator possibly have against—"

"The Last Judgment." Matthew took a deep breath. "My mother told me about that. How can God gather together all the body parts for glory if they're not there, in one place where they're supposed to be?"

"Talk about being literal-minded!" Cornwall snorted. "You think God isn't powerful enough to collect a few puny missing skulls from the shelves of my collection? You think the God who made man to begin with isn't powerful enough to put all the pieces back together again? Answer me that one, boy."

"Well—" Matthew's thoughts swirled like the mists around him. He finally burst out, "But my whole entire family is buried out here somewhere! Maybe even in Potter's Field. They took them away and I don't know where!"

The doctor's voice softened. "It's not your family we're going after, son. I swear to you. I know precisely who I'm after, and he's long gone. It will be the last of my general collection, before I move on to specifics."

"I still don't approve, sir. It's madness. I can't!"

"Hum." The doctor stood facing him through

the fog. "Hum. But you approve of being off the streets, don't you. You approve of being fed and clothed."

Matthew squirmed. "Yes, sir."

"And I've fed and clothed you rather well thus far, haven't I? Even begun your education?"

"Yes, sir," Matthew had to agree.

"And I haven't shown any other signs of mistreating you?"

"Oh, no, sir. You've been very kind!"

The doctor forged on. "I haven't shown any other signs of peculiar behavior, or of madness, have I?"

That gave Matthew pause. The whole entire phrenology business did have a certain air of craziness about it, still . . .

"Well, then." The doctor's voice turned hearty again. "Well, then, if you choose to continue to be fed and clothed, and to continue to have a roof over your head, I suppose you'll just have to trust me. Won't you?"

"I suppose so, sir." Matthew's voice was grudging, and it made him feel a little bad considering how truly decent the doctor had been so far, yet . . .

Asa B. Cornwall pulled at his arm again. "The night isn't getting any younger. And we've still a distance to go. Come along, lad."

Skunked. Slammed and skunked quite thoroughly, Matthew grasped his digging equipment more firmly and followed.

"The gate's locked. Bolted from the inside." The doctor's whisper was tinged with dismay. He studied the stiff wrought iron that twisted into spearlike points above his head. "We'll have to climb over the wall."

Matthew nodded numbly. During the last half mile the fog had thickened into the heaviest he'd ever experienced. Now it shifted almost bodily about and before him, making it nearly impossible to see more than a foot or two ahead. He took a tentative step. To one side of the gate patches of shapes broke through the cottony vapors, black against black. Some of those shapes were cut stones piled upon each other in a wall that seemed guardian to the ends of the earth. For all he knew, it could be the end of the earth beyond. A sheer drop into nothingness. But when he tossed his sack in a high arc, he heard it thud to the ground on the far side.

"Up you go, lad."

There was nothing else to do. Matthew fit fingers and toes into waiting cracks and hoisted himself. There was a ledge atop the wall with brief flat spaces between jagged points. When he'd reached it and twisted to fling his legs over the far side, he wedged his chest into one of the narrow gaps and leaned back down to help the doctor. This was a more difficult task by far. Satchel bumping against his body, Asa B. Cornwall stretched to grasp Matthew's hand, then struggled to elevate his girth. He huffed and he puffed. He nearly pulled Matthew down upon his head.

Finally, he relinquished his grip and called up. "Now you know why I advertised for you, lad. The mind might be nimble, but the flesh lags far behind. See if you can't open that gate from the inside."

Matthew murmured agreement and slid from the top over the back side of the wall. After gaining the solid ground he felt blindly for his tools. Finding them, he dragged his free hand along the stone wall toward the gate. Once there, it was simple enough to lift the iron bar. He pulled the heavy gate slightly ajar. The creak cut through the night.

"Doctor? Sir?"

"Here!" The voice came from behind.

Matthew jumped and waited for his heart to slow again. "I thought you were—"

"Don't think at all in here," snapped the doctor. "And don't utter another word!"

Cornwall took the lead, with Matthew following almost on his heels. To do otherwise would be to lose himself in this place till morning. If dawn ever broke again. He had doubts about that. He had doubts about everything except the overwhelming fear that this night would never end.

Meanwhile, the doctor navigated his way through a maze of low mounds and sagging crosses. The white fog swirled around them, taking on terrifying, otherworldly shapes. It was cold, yet Matthew felt sweat on his brow. *If I only survive this*, he promised himself, *I'll never, ever set foot in a cemetery again. I'll never, ever—*

"This is it!" the doctor hissed. He leaned closer to a derelict cross, then pulled out a matchstick and struck the head upon its rough length. "Yes," he continued. "Henry Bedlow. Resting here entirely too quietly these forty-odd years. Well, your time has come, scoundrel. Mother Carey's chickens never forgot you, and neither have I."

"Chickens?" Matthew asked. "What have chickens got to do with—"

"Quiet!" Cornwall blew out the match. "Start digging before we hear the crow of the cock!"

Matthew emptied the sack, raised the pick, and aimed it toward the grave.

Thunk.

His new career as a grave robber had begun.

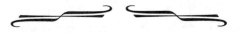

Several feet down, Matthew shed his scarf and jacket. After another foot, his shirt followed. Sweat and the earthy pungency of damp dirt surrounded him. He felt he would choke. Even knowing that the grave's occupant was a rogue didn't help to ease his dread. He sliced the shovel through another foot of the soil and continued tossing the dirt out of the grave as he sank lower and lower. Above him, Asa B. Cornwall paced.

"Nothing yet?" Cornwall's face hovered over him.

Matthew had a sudden urge to throw the next shovel full of dirt over the doctor. He didn't. He reached down once more, every muscle in his body screaming from the strain. He stabbed the earth yet again. The shovel made a new sound.

"Sir? This might be—"

But the doctor was already in the hole with him. "Quickly now. We don't need the whole coffin uncovered. Just the part toward the cross. The head."

Matthew scraped a spot clean. The doctor

shoved him aside to grasp the pick himself. In a moment there was a crunch of disintegrating wood. Tossing the pick aside, Cornwall tore at the decaying shards with his bare hands. Then another match was struck.

"Hah! There he lies. One would almost say in the flesh, but as that is far from the case—"

Matthew refused to even glance at the doctor's treasure. He'd done enough. He pulled himself to the top of the hole and felt for his shirt and jacket. But the doctor remained in the grave, talking now to himself. Or was it to the head?

" 'That skull had a tongue in it, and could sing once. . . . Alas, poor Yorick!' "

"I thought his name was Bedlow," Matthew called down.

"Barbarian. Throw me my satchel."

Good. They'd be clear of here soon. Matthew reached for the bag, then stiffened at a new sound. "Sir?" he quavered.

"What now!"

"I hear voices."

"Help me out of here!"

Matthew pulled with all his might while the doctor scrabbled in the loosened dirt. He nearly floored Matthew when he flew out, but he was out. "Grab the tools. Quickly."

"But aren't we going to close up the grave again? Tidy it?"

"No time."

Cornwall rushed into the mists, clutching his prize to his chest. Matthew grabbed for the tools and followed. Halfway to the gate a torch broke through the fetid atmosphere. Matthew halted his flight to pause behind a tree, mesmerized by the light. As it grew closer his mouth gaped. The torch was held by the most villainous looking man he'd ever laid eyes on: long straggly hair floated over filthy garments, and a jagged scar ran down one side of his face—from a markedly broad and low brow. Behind him were two others equal in frightfulness. They were carrying shovels, ropes, and sacks.

An arm reached out and snatched at Matthew. He nearly screamed till he realized it was the doctor.

"*There* are your body snatchers," Cornwall growled. "Going after fresh meat for the medical students to dissect. Do I look like one of them?"

Matthew only choked and bolted headlong for the gate.

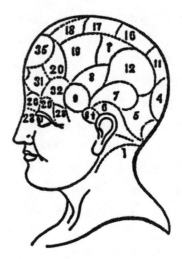

CHAPTER FOUR

WHEN MATTHEW FINALLY WOKE THE NEXT MORNING, he staggered from his cot to gaze out a window. The dawn had come and day had broken—but grayly. It was raining steadily, relentlessly. As he stared at the mournful, heavy sky, he absently ran a hand through his hair, then rubbed his face. He pulled his fingers away from his nose as if scorched. Heaven help him, he still smelled like the cemetery, like Potter's Field. It was an unclean smell, bringing back all the horrors of the night. A bath. He had to have a bath!

"Doctor?" He spun around in search of the man, but all he found waiting was that skull. Henry Bedlow sat atop the table grinning like the miscreant he was.

"Aargh!" Matthew lunged for the disembodied head with every intention of smashing it to the floor, or maybe tossing it from the fifth floor window. He had it in his grasp—

"Ah, you're up!" Cornwall trotted around the screen from the studio, a picture of contentment. "I see you're admiring our Henry. A fine specimen, isn't he? What I won't be able to learn about the mind gone astray from him! Although he could use a little tidying up first." The doctor reached out for the dirt-encrusted object and Matthew wordlessly dropped it into his hands. "Since you seem to be uncertain about your next chore, why don't I assign Henry to you? It will be excellent practice."

Matthew hugged his arms to his chest to make his sudden goose bumps disappear. Digging up Henry had been one thing, but to have to make his closer acquaintance . . . "Would that be wise, sir? You'd allow me to touch one of your *specimens* without proper training?"

"Nothing to it, lad. Nothing to it. I generally use a dental pick and a soft painter's brush for the cleaning process. Never water. The tools should be lying around here somewhere. Only go gently. Exceptionally gently. Bones are more delicate than anyone imagines. Especially old bones."

"Sir?"

The doctor looked up at the quaver in Matthew's voice. "What is it, lad?"

"Might I have a bath first, sir?"

Matthew spent the rest of that rainy Sunday hunkered over Henry Bedlow's cranium. Once he'd gotten the knack of using the fine pick to chisel bits of hardened dirt from nooks and crannies, he was surprised by how restful the work was. He could let his mind wander, let it wonder upon what Henry's crime had been. Robbery? Murder? And how could either be connected to chickens?

Then his thoughts flew to what could possibly happen to himself if he were cast back into the streets again. Cornwall seemed cheerful enough today, but last night's mission hadn't really been discussed. Matthew's reluctance to do the work had not been discussed. What if the doctor was upset with him? Plum jobs were not exactly easy to find. No job was for someone his age, someone who hadn't officially begun an apprenticeship. He

knew that from hard personal experience.
Begging to run errands and shovel snow and
sweep shops hadn't kept his stomach full all winter. If he didn't continue to please Dr. Cornwall,
back on the streets is where he'd find himself.
From there, who knows? Out of desperation he
could turn into another Henry Bedlow.

Trembling from that thought, Matthew tore his
eyes from the skull. The work was no longer restful. He began studying the two charts Cornwall
was unrolling under the dim illumination drift-
ing from the studio skylight. What now?

The doctor hummed to himself while bustling
around. He finished propping up the charts and
stood back to admire their effect. Then he spoke.
"Having passed your initiation last night with fly-
ing colors—"

"I did?" Matthew interrupted with shock. "I
passed?"

"You survived Potter's Field, didn't you?
Successfully, too." Cornwall beamed upon
Bedlow. "Unlike our subject here, you kept your
head square upon your shoulders and your wits
about you. I couldn't ask for more from my new
permanent apprentice and official assistant."

In spite of himself, in spite of everything,
Matthew smiled.

"Thank you, sir."

He blew out his breath in a great heave of relief. *Permanent*, the doctor said. He had a permanent job, a permanent roof over his head. He'd just have to remember to have more faith in God and the Last Judgment. Watching how attached Cornwall had become to Henry Bedlow, Matthew strongly suspected this skull would not be the last to join the doctor's collection.

Asa B. Cornwall smiled back. "So it's time you began learning the jargon of the trade, my boy," he continued. "While I return to revising my manuscript you may meditate upon the phreno-logical organs, the thirty-five distinct faculties of the mind. I'll expect you to have them memorized before too long." With Matthew's future settled, Dr. Cornwall trotted back to his *magnum opus*.

Matthew brushed a bit of grave dirt from his fingers while he studied the first chart. It was a side view of the human head, blessedly cloaked in flesh. The shaved skull was marked off in squares, rectangles, ovals, and more irregular shapes. Within each shape was printed the name of the "faculty" allotted to that section of the head. Interestingly enough, Cautiousness and Combativeness seemed to hold a lion's share of the space. He glanced over to the second chart. It

showed the same male head, the same side view.
But the sections were filled with the numbers that
corresponded to their attributes.

"So," he mumbled to himself, "that would
make Cautiousness number twelve, and
Combativeness number five."

Matthew memorized and considered while
chipping away at Henry Bedlow. After an hour
Cornwall wandered back into the studio rubbing
his eyes. "How's Henry coming?"

"Fine, sir." Matthew pushed back from the skull
while the doctor bent for his inspection. "But I
had a few questions for you about these charts."

"Yes?"

"About this faculties numbering system? Is
there any significance to the order?"

Cornwall plopped onto the floor beside him.
"Excellent question. Absolutely perceptive of
you!" He pointed to the closest chart. "The lower
numbers concern feelings, the middle senti-
ments, while the highest numbers refer to the
intellectual faculties—senses and knowing. Take
Henry here." He picked up the half-cleaned skull
and pointed to the area directly above where the
ear should have been. "See this enlarged lump?"

Matthew nodded.

"That's Bedlow's Destructiveness organ.

Number six, under the order of Feelings, genus number one, Propensities. It shows a tendency to passion and rage. Among the lower animals it distinguishes carnivorousness. Rarely seen such a big one." His finger moved half an inch to the right. "And directly next to it. This other bump? Combativeness. Number five under 'Feelings.' That's enlarged, too." His finger slipped slightly lower beneath the area of the ear. "See this bruised section? That's Amativeness. Number one. Appropriate. Very appropriate."

"Amativeness?" Matthew asked.

"Stands for love, my boy. The propensity to love. From the Latin, *amo, amas, amat*—I love, you love, he loves, and so forth." He settled the skull back upon the floor. "So there! He was obviously controlled by his feelings. Loving unwisely was poor Henry's downfall."

Matthew scratched his head. That didn't sound nearly as wicked as murder or robbery. "What did Henry actually do all those years ago?"

"Seduced a pretty young thing and was brought to trial for his efforts."

"And?"

"He was acquitted. But the young lady's father had other thoughts on the subject, and so did the father's mates. He gathered together a huge mob that rioted over the city for three nights after Henry was set free."

"Where do the chickens you mentioned last night come in? I don't understand about the chickens!"

Cornwall laughed. "I was a boy then, younger than you, and I sat up in a tree by Mother Carey's boardinghouse—the place where the assignation occurred—watching the proceedings, watching the mob destroy the house while all of Mother Carey's chickens were dispersed to the winds. Such a cackling I'll never forget! So I always seem to think of Henry's troubles and chickens as somehow interconnected."

Matthew still wasn't sure he understood. He looked on the bones with a little more compassion. Maybe the man had truly been in love and it was all just a big misunderstanding. "Then what happened to Henry?"

"Well, I guess he was caught, wasn't he?"

Cornwall struggled to his feet and Matthew took pick to skull once more.

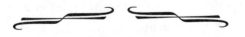

A week passed by and Matthew and the doctor were eating porridge again. Matthew now understood what that meant—they were once more without funds. Penniless, in fact. The largesse of Mrs. Higginbotham and friends had disappeared into their new wardrobes. But what was the use of fancy clothes without clients to show them off to? He sipped from his cup of water, then cleared his throat. Cornwall's head popped up from his bowl.

"Did you say something, Matthew?"

"No, sir, but I'm about to."

The doctor pulled his napkin to his lips. "Speak up, then, lad."

"It's about our current state of affairs, sir."

"What current state of affairs?"

"That's precisely it, Doctor. We have no current state of affairs. No clients, either. Not even Mrs. Higginbotham!"

"Oh, Elsie. She's gone off to visit her daughter in Philadelphia for a few months. She mentioned that most specifically during her last consultation."

Matthew groaned.

"What was that for? I didn't think you were that fond of the silly woman!"

"She may be silly, sir, but she kept us in beefsteak. Apple pie, too." He licked a clump of oatmeal from his spoon, wishing it were a bite of Mrs. Higginbotham's fabulous pie, then set it down with resolution. "We've got to do something about drumming up new patients, sir."

Asa B. Cornwall glanced toward a bin sitting behind the stove. "No need to fret. We've got at least a month's worth of oatmeal on hand yet, lad."

"Exactly!"

The doctor ignored his comment. "And I'm really quite deeply immersed in my manuscript at the moment. Another month without interruptions and I'll have the first half completed. That will free me up for some heavy thinking about how to proceed with research for the second half—"

"I know you're working hard, sir," Matthew broke in, "but I've cleaned and polished everything in sight. Plus I've begun reading through your library—"

"Excellent! Quite excellent! Can't think of a better use of your time at this point. Remember to make a list of questions that may occur to you in the course of your studies. Present them to me at my leisure and I'll answer them."

Matthew shook his head in frustration. "But the rains have finally stopped, sir. After a complete week of totally foul weather—"

"Even better! Get out and take the air. A young boy like you needs lots of fresh air!"

Matthew stared at his employer. "You don't mind? I'm supposed to be working for you!"

"And you are, you are. That doesn't mean I need to crack the whip over you once an hour." Cornwall touched Matthew's arm. "Relax, lad. I appreciate your strongly developed faculty of Conscientiousness, but you needn't overdo it. There's something to be said for simple companionship, yes?"

That's when Matthew realized that even with a roof over his head, the doctor had been lonely, too. For the first time he wondered about Dr. ABC's past.

"Sir? Did you ever have a family?"

"Eh?"

"You know, a mother and father, little sisters and brothers . . ."

Cornwall patted at the strands atop his head, rearranging them. "Everyone has to start somewhere, don't they?"

"Did you ever have a family of your own?" Matthew pushed on.

"You mean a wife? Where would I find time for a wife, lad? I've been studying hard practically since Mother Carey's chickens spread their wings." He stopped. "Come to think about it, I suppose Mother Carey's chickens were a defining moment in my life."

"How could that be, sir?"

"Well, when they flew the coop, they pecked me out of my perch in the tree. I fell on my head, got properly trounced by the mob, and decided then and there that I didn't approve of either mobs or the mentality that went with them. That's when I took to books. I determined that my goal in life would be to become a thinking man. As a thinking man, perhaps I could find out what made others think, and thus eventually better understand their actions. Phrenology is the natural culmination of that goal."

Matthew blinked. "That's the most interesting story I ever heard. It explains Henry, too."

"I suppose it does." The doctor nodded. "Satisfied?"

"Yes, sir."

Then and there Matthew determined to seek his own goal in life. For the moment he kept it simple: keeping his stomach full by hanging on to his permanent job. But to keep his job truly permanent, the doctor's business had to improve. He needed to learn how to improve it, and firmly set his mind to accomplishing that new task.

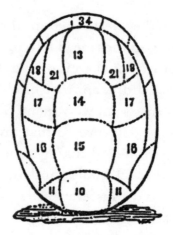

Chapter Five

THE NEXT DAY WAS GLORIOUS. FORTIFIED BY HIS morning bowl of porridge, Matthew set off on his idea-finding mission. He rambled all over the city inspecting shops and signs, pausing for the free entertainment of barkers hawking everything from oysters to cloth to knives. It was on Nassau Street that he found his true inspiration. Strange that he hadn't noticed this place of business during his earlier days wandering the streets. But then, up to a few weeks before, the word *phrenology* had never entered his consciousness. Here it was, though, printed in huge letters right over a streetfront shop:

> FOWLER BROTHERS
> ## PHRENOLOGY EMPORIUM
> ENTER FOR INEXPENSIVE CONSULTATIONS

A little bell rang as Matthew pushed open the door. He quickly took in the now familiar surroundings of the phrenological world: bust-filled shelves, garishly colored reading charts. There didn't seem to be any genuine skulls on hand, though. Maybe Dr. Cornwall was ahead of the profession on that score.

"May I be of service?"

Matthew turned toward the heavily bearded man just emerging from a curtained-off room to the rear.

"Perhaps you'll be in need of a reading as a job reference?" the gentleman continued. "I get quite a few lads your age needing references."

"Er. How much would that be, sir?"

"Lowest prices in town. A mere dollar for a basic character reading. Three dollars if you wish it written up in chart form for your employer.

And with that"—he reached over to a nearby table—"with that, you get the Fowler brothers' own book on the subject, autographed by myself, as well as inscribed with your name and your attainments in the various faculties." He smiled, revealing a row of very well-kept teeth. "Phrenology is the wave of the future, young man. With it, we will revolutionize the world! Now, if you'd just like to step into my reading parlor—"

"Thank you, sir," Matthew finally managed to stammer, "but I'll have to return with the money in hand."

"You do that. Best investment you'll ever make. And when you come back, ask for me personally. Orson Squire Fowler."

"I certainly shall, Mr. Fowler." Matthew escaped to trot back home, his head suddenly brimming with ideas. *Home.* He smiled. Now that he'd found one again, he wasn't about to let either himself or Dr. Cornwall lose it.

Matthew needed seed money for his grand plans. In order to acquire that, he dressed himself in his new suit of clothes, carefully arranged the stock of his cravat, and made a stab at taming his dark curls. He ignored the doctor blissfully immersed in his manuscript, but patted Henry Bedlow's freshly varnished pate for luck. Then he set back down the four flights of stairs. He knew now what he had to do. If hawking worked for oysters on the half shell, why not for phrenology?

Outside the doorway, he took a stance and murmured, *"Remember the goal."* Taking a deep breath, he began gathering the passing crowds.

"Phrenologize our nation!"

He cleared his throat and upped the volume.

"Reform the world! Step right up, ladies and gentlemen. Children, too! Don't miss your golden opportunity to turn your life around." Half a dozen passersby had already paused. He stared straight into the closest pair of eyes.

"Yes, ladies and gentlemen, it's all in your heads. Right there in your heads! You only need to have them read to learn your true potential!"

Matthew stopped to inspect his listeners. They seemed curious. Good. "Dr. ABC is the best phrenologist in town! Dr. ABC is the thinking man's phrenologist! He's got the best prices in town, too, ladies and gentlemen! Only one slim dollar for a general reading. But if you want the works, he'll give you that, too!"

"How much is the works?" A man asked.

Matthew studied him. He looked a little tipsy.

Still, if he had money in his pockets . . . "Only three dollars for you, sir. Turn your life around right now. This very day!"

"I can turn my life around in the nearest tavern for an entire week for that price, boy!"

"True enough, sir. But where is the drink leading you? Tell me that! Dr. ABC can give you the ABCs to changing everything. For this small investment you'll be able to save three dollars a week for the rest of your life!"

The man considered long and hard. Then he staggered toward Matthew. "Fair enough. Lead on, my boy."

Matthew turned wary. "You've got the coins, sir?"

A pocket was jingled. "Certainly got the coins. Now, will you have them or no?"

Matthew grabbed the man's arm as the rest of the crowd slipped away. With some effort he shoved him up four flights of stairs, his mind whirring steadily the entire trip. Five minutes was all it had taken. Easier than oysters. If he were to get some handbills printed and distributed, and maybe convince the doctor to do up a little pamphlet like the Fowler brothers had . . .

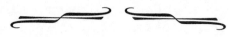

"I don't approve of these rock-bottom prices you've foisted on me, Matthew Morrissey!"

Matthew sat at the small table tallying up the results of a week's worth of their new program. He glanced up. "Stop fussing, sir. We've got to be competitive. Most of the new clients go for the full reading at three dollars a head, anyway, and you've been getting faster at it—"

"Faster, faster," Cornwall grumbled. "And is faster better? Some of the charm disappears, boy. The fun begins to dissipate, too."

Matthew ignored the complaints. "We've been averaging thirty dollars a day for five entire days. When was the last time you had one hundred and fifty dollars in hand?"

"Currently in your hand," the doctor groused. He made a move toward the neatly stacked piles of coins. Matthew held him off. "Not yet. We've got to invest some of this in order to make more."

"Invest? I'd like to invest the money, right enough, in a haunch of beef, or a leg of lamb. Why are we still eating porridge?"

Matthew's lips twitched. "You yourself told me it was the most healthful of foods, sir. No, with this nest egg we ought to plan our future. The first thing I'll need to do is visit a signmaker. I've already spoken to the landlord. For a modest fee he'll let you hang a shingle out front so your clients will know you're here. Word of mouth isn't good enough, Doctor. Not when it includes four flights of stairs."

"But, but—" Dr. Cornwall spluttered.

Matthew overrode the protest. "That means I can spend less time working the street for patients, and more time on organizational details."

Cornwall threw up his hands. "Such as what?"

"Such as having booklets and charts printed to hand out to customers, the same as the Fowler brothers do. I've been studying their methods, sir. I even went back for one of their three-dollar readings—"

"And?" broke in the doctor.

This time the boy grinned. "You've got much more style with patients, sir. Also, Mr. Fowler got my analysis all wrong. He said I was strong on Ideality and had to watch out for dwelling in the regions of fancy and neglecting the duties of life."

Cornwall snorted.

"Nevertheless," Matthew pressed on. "Nevertheless, we've got to get into *practical* phrenology in a big way. That's where the money is. Did you know that the Fowlers are training apprentices to go on the road? Mr. Fowler bragged about it to me while he was doing my analysis. They're heading out to upstate New York, and even to the West! And the brothers will be taking a percentage of all those apprentices' profits."

"But I have no desire to become a traveling circus, Matthew! Nor a stationary one, either, for that matter. When I choose to travel, it will be for a loftier purpose."

Matthew sat back. "What sort of loftier purpose?"

Asa B. Cornwall stared longingly at the money pile. "If we were to actually save some of that . . . Add a little more . . ." He rubbed his hands and paced around the table. "I just never conceived there might be funds enough for my greatest dream. I fantasized, surely I did, but—"

"What dream, sir?"

Cornwall flung out his arms. "Why properly researching the second half of my *magnum opus*, of course! The specifics! The specifics that will get me inside the heads of the most interesting people, the greatest thinkers of history! Such research requires travel, lad. To strange and distant places." His arms dropped and he began wringing his hands. "If only you could guarantee that we might make this much consistently, for long enough to build up a little war chest, I might be able to put up with the interim indignities. It's not as if I've been stinting on my new patients. I have been giving them honest readings. . . ." He ceased his pacing. "But now you tell me we must waste all of this on fripperies—"

"Not all of it, sir. But we have to let people know we're here. You've got to spend money to make money. And most of it, like the sign, we'll only have to pay for once." He smiled with satisfaction. "Then we can really begin to give the Fowler brothers some competition."

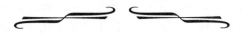

Matthew was quite proud of the new sign. Beside Dr. ABC's name, title, and services there was a neat red arrow pointing up the staircase. But the truly original addition—which the Fowlers did not have on their sign—was a gloriously colored image of a phrenological head chart, complete with inscribed organ names. He tapped in the last square nail and stood back in admiration.

"There!" he exclaimed to Dr. Cornwall, who'd been dragged from his manuscript for the unveiling. "How about that!"

"Hum," the doctor muttered. "Hum." He

rubbed at his jowls. "It's not bad. Quite comely, in fact." He glanced at Matthew. "There wasn't any extra room for my portrait, I suppose? Just a simple head view—"

"Eureka!"

Matthew and the doctor spun around at the exclamation.

"Eureka!" a passerby repeated. "Could this be the very Asa B. Cornwall whose illuminating article was published in the *Proceedings of the Phrenological Society of Washington*?"

The doctor stared at the stranger, then found his tongue. "It is, but that was back in 1828—"

"Time never dulls brilliance, my good sir. Your report on the skull of that executed murderer was inspiring. Allow me to introduce myself." A bony hand shot out from a tall body, slim and supple as a sapling, yet curiously aged. "Charles Tombe, a fellow enthusiast."

Cornwall gasped. "Not *the* Tombe, the Tombe from Britain who's been lecturing in New England?"

"In the flesh, Doctor, in the flesh," he chuckled.

"But I've followed your experiments! To actually meet you—"

"Not only meet," Tombe replied. "Such a fortuitous event suggests the fates intended more. Perhaps we might compare notes? At your convenience, of course."

Matthew glanced back and forth between the two. He was unsure what to make of the incident. Now he saw Dr. Cornwall actually blush.

"A fellow scholar! At last someone with whom to discuss my almost completed manuscript!" He waved toward the stairs. "What better time than the present?" Cornwall stopped. "That is, if you're presently at leisure . . ."

"All the time in the world, my dear fellow." Tombe struck his walking stick hard against the paving in emphasis. "All the time in the world."

The doctor beamed at the response. "Then please follow me, Tombe. My studio may be humble, but it is up in the world!" He turned to Matthew. "Fetch us some fresh cream and buns, like a good lad. And I won't be seeing any patients today."

"Yes, sir. No, sir." Matthew retrieved the hammer and scrambled to obey.

Much later that night the doctor sat at the table amongst the disarray of his manuscript. Charles Tombe had spent the day studying and comparing it to his own work. Cornwall was still recovering from the experience.

"Brains, Matthew. He's been dissecting actual brains."

"Brains, sir? How could he do that?"

"He keeps them in jars, floating in preservatives. Tombe says he's got hundreds in his collection already."

Matthew got that old midnight cemetery feeling. He choked on the queasiness rising from his stomach. "But that means he'd have to be working with fresh cadavers—"

"Precisely!" Cornwall's fist slammed onto the tabletop. "Dissection hasn't been illegal in Britain since 1831. Oh, the boundless possibilities that allows—"

"You wouldn't . . ." Matthew gulped back his gorge again. "You wouldn't want to do the same, would you, sir?"

The doctor's eyes focused on his strewn papers. "Hard to say. It's a totally different direction. . . . And I do think my skull theory is quite unique in and of itself, even if Tombe did dash quite a large bucket of cold water over it toward the end of our discussions. After starting off on such a positive note . . ." Cornwall shivered. "Iced water, in point of fact." He stared up at Matthew beseechingly. "Am I on the wrong track, lad? Is my life's work to be for naught?"

Matthew bristled at the thought of the overbearing, cadaverous Tombe treating his master's ideas the way he had. He bristled at the very idea of Tombe. The man had kept him running errands for his comfort the entire day, with never a thank-you.

"What right has he to be invited into our home, and then end up insulting you? I don't care how important he is. You should stick to your guns, sir."

"Yes," Cornwall finally conceded. "There's room for more than one approach in the discipline. But to have actually had the opportunity to discuss such topics with a great mind! As an equal!"

"Well, I should hope so, sir," Matthew continued his objections. "You're anyone's equal, and better, too!"

"You didn't care for Tombe much, did you, lad?" Cornwall didn't wait for the answer. "But I appreciate your loyalty." He began gathering the manuscript. "It was a thought-provoking day. I'll be seeing clients again tomorrow, Master Morrissey. As many as you can find for me. We'll need to begin saving money. Lots of money. My skulls just might refute Tombe's brain theory."

He set down his stacked papers to pull at his collar. "Has it suddenly gotten warm in here? Strange how the man's ice has lit a fire under me again. So much work to do! My mind is feeling hot enough to burst into flames!"

Matthew opened all the studio windows as wide as possible, then fetched a cool glass of water for the doctor. He knew it was merely a figure of speech, but he was uneasy with the effect the long visit with that Englishman had had on his master and only friend.

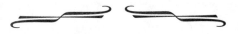

Time passed and their war chest grew. Then strange events began to occur. The first was a mysterious midnight visit.

The new sign had been in place for several weeks, and Matthew was lying awake congratulating himself once more on its effectiveness, even without the pamphlets, which Corwall had vetoed. Now that nights were getting warmer and he needn't be in such close proximity to the little stove, he'd taken to dragging his cot into the studio at bedtime to escape the doctor's steady snoring. Another consideration was that he could center his bed directly under the skylights and see the stars.

This night, though, he'd been following the brightness of a three-quarter moon as it majestically moved across the arc of blackness. Fighting back sleep while watching, his mind wove drowsily between his new life and his old one. Dr. Cornwall stirring the morning porridge turned into his mother stooping before the fireplace, performing the same task. Dr. Cornwall at the table with his manuscript became Matthew's father sitting at a larger table carefully reading his daily newspaper. Back and forth, in and out, while the moon progressed to the next window.

Until he heard the sound.

He shot up, tossing a blanket from his body. Nights on the street had taught him wariness.

Yes. It came again.

A slight scratch on the studio door. As if someone were toying with the lock. Matthew soundlessly crept to the door and laid his ear against it. The noises intensified. He put his hand on the knob and jerked.

"Curses!"

A darkly draped shape spat out the single word before fleeing. Matthew pursued the figure through the darkness of the long hallway. Lunging out, he grabbed onto a cloak. Put off balance, the figure went half-stumbling, half-falling down the stairs. Outraged oaths echoed through four flights.

Matthew listened with satisfaction, waiting for the slam of the street door. When it came he retraced his steps through the hallway, waving away a curious miasma that seemed to hover there. Safely inside the studio again, he carefully positioned the heavy armchair against the door and crawled back beneath his blankets. The next thing he knew it was morning, and there was Dr. Cornwall bearing a fresh cup of coffee.

"What's all this, lad?" Cornwall squinted from Matthew's rumpled blankets to the armchair—propped door.

Matthew rubbed his eyes and accepted the offering. "I'll have to visit the ironmonger's for a strong bolt. We had an uninvited visitor last night. I think I frightened him off. At least I seem to remember someone blaspheming all the way down the stairs."

Cornwall's shaggy eyebrows rose. "And what would anyone be expecting to steal from a phrenological studio?"

"I'm not sure, sir. Not sure at all."

Matthew purchased and even installed the new bolt that very day, between patients. That night he settled into his cot under the skylight with a certain sense of satisfaction and security. He managed to keep his eyes open long enough to see the three-quarter moon grown larger. Then he dreamed.

Dr. Cornwall was in his dreams again, but instead of stirring porridge or studying his manuscript, the man was crouched over a series of jars. Matthew felt himself creep silently ever closer and closer as if being pulled toward those jars. It was their color: they glowed with a wild, putrid green phosphorescence. And their contents. Masses of knotted-up snakes. Were they pulsating? Yes, and beating time to their movements, beating like a drum, or like careful, consistent footsteps . . .

Matthew jerked awake all at once. *Footsteps.* On the roof over his head. His eyes widened. Something was blocking the light of the moon. No, *someone.* Someone was overhead, and he was staring through the skylight!

Matthew yelled. Cornwall was with him in an instant, shaking his shoulders.

"What in heaven's name is the matter, lad? A nightmare?"

"Yes . . . and no." He pointed at the skylight.

"What?" The doctor's head creaked up. "What did you see?"

"Someone trying to get in, sir." He shook his head to clear away the last of the sleep. "Through the only other possible entry."

"Hum." Cornwall rubbed at his bald head. "Gone now, of course. Your shriek could have roused the dead, never mind scare off a simple burglar."

Matthew was now fully awake. He stared at the doctor draped in nightshirt and moonlight. "That's two nights in a row, sir."

"I noticed." Cornwall craned his neck toward the moon again. "But my first response still applies. What could we possibly have that someone else wants this badly?"

Matthew found out later the next morning when he went out to purchase bread and cheese for their midday meal. It had been a slow morning. Not a single client had arrived. He'd marked it down to the lovely early June day until he pushed the door open onto the building's stone stoop and automatically turned around to admire his sign.

It wasn't there!

Matthew rubbed his eyes, then walked right up to the wall where it had been. Yes, there were the holes from the nails still denting the brick. He glanced down. Here, in fact, was one of the nails, torn out and twisted. He picked it up. Had one of the doctor's patients become angry with his analysis? Had their late-night visitor taken his revenge on the sign when he couldn't retrieve anything of greater value? Or—a fresh thought— had someone become upset by the doctor's thriving new business? Shoving the nail in a pocket, Matthew set off double time for Nassau Street.

A few steps from the corner of Nassau and Matthew's goal—the Fowlers' Phrenological Emporium—a distinctive smell halted him in his tracks. That smell . . . The same smell had surrounded him in the hallway outside the studio after the first burglary attempt. It was out of place in the bright sunshine of the day. It was a musty odor, connected in his mind with dense fogs, and moist earth, and . . . cemeteries!

Suddenly alert, Matthew edged into the alley behind Nassau Street. Someone was there, working his way between piles of garbage and empty barrels. He seemed to be heading for the center of the block, where the Fowler brothers might have their rear entrance.

Matthew hid behind one of the piles. He put his eye to a gap in the ribbing of a barrel and peered through. The man had reached his destination and was knocking on a hidden door. As he turned to glance suspiciously over his shoulder, a ray of sunshine squarely caught his hulking profile and boldly illuminated it: the brow was broad and low, and a long jagged scar moved from eyebrow to chin. Shoulder length, scraggly hair completed the picture.

"The body snatcher!" Matthew gasped.

Matthew clapped a hand over his mouth as the villain spun full circle. Having no intention of learning what might happen next, Matthew raced from the alley toward the safety of Broadway and Dr. Cornwall.

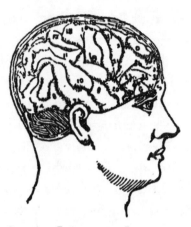

PHRENO-CENTRES OF IDEATION

CHAPTER SIX

"IT's a sign!" Asa B. Cornwall exclaimed.

"No, it's *our* sign, stolen!" Matthew impatiently explained once more. "Torn right off the wall! Undoubtedly by that body snatcher, in league with the Fowlers—"

The doctor pushed him into the empty armchair, then stood over him. "Will you calm down for a moment and pay attention, boy? Your evidence is circumstantial at best. Merely sighting one of this city's many lowlifes—"

"A *particular* lowlife!" Matthew insisted. "With a connection to the business. Cemeteries, after all—"

Cornwall overrode his comment. "Merely sighting this person in the vicinity of our competitors is insufficient proof of anything. Besides, I'm of the opinion that a larger mind than the Fowlers' own—even collectively—is behind our recent troubles, and—"

"A larger mind such as Charles Tombe's?" Matthew asked.

"Nonsense," Cornwall shot back. "You just never took to him. Tombe is a scholar and a gentleman. A scholar and a gentleman would never sink so low. No, our troubles arise from a greater conspiracy—"

"What kind of a conspiracy?" Matthew interrupted once more.

The doctor paused. "I'm uncertain at the moment," he admitted. "Some sort of secret society. Rosicrucians, perhaps? They're deeply interested in enlightenment, but are Luddites at heart, strongly opposed to serious, *modern* scientific disciplines. I wouldn't put it past them to try to destroy my evidence." He shook his head. "I'm sure time will answer all." Cornwall waved off all the other questions Matthew was ready to raise. "In the meantime, our missing sign is also the sign I've been waiting for."

Matthew tugged at his thick curls in frustration. "But—"

"In view of the message being sent, we've got to act, but we've got to think, too." Cornwall began pacing back and forth under the studio's skylights. "First thing, find my traveling bags. They're tucked under something somewhere. Fill them up with our new clothes and my manuscript. My instruments and your lesson books. Our war fund." He stopped. "And throw the tools into that sack, too."

"Which tools?"

"You know perfectly well which tools. The first half of my *magnum opus* is as finished as it's going to be. I've just been moving commas and semicolons around for the last week anyway. The time has come for Part Two."

"Part Two?" Matthew knew he was beginning to sound like a parrot, but it was the only response that came with the sudden crash of his carefully organized life.

"The second part of my book, and my life, too. I've been fussing over it all in my mind ever since Charles Tombe's visit. I needed but a catalyst, and that's how I've chosen to interpret this series of events."

Matthew pushed out of the armchair and gestured around the room. "What about the studio?"

"We'll pay the landlord some advance rent and just lock it up. If someone—or group—wants my casts and skulls this badly, I say welcome. They've served their purpose." Cornwall took in his small world. "Except for Henry. Pack Henry Bedlow up, as well. He might come in handy."

"But, but—"

"No more buts, Matthew Morrissey. It's the *specifics* that will rule us from hence." Dr. ABC made the declaration with absolute finality.

"Fetch us some tickets, lad. I'll watch the luggage."

Matthew set down an overstuffed leather satchel and the sack of digging equipment in front of a three-story tenement that called itself Kit Burns's Sportsmen's Hall. It sat by the waterfront in one of the seedier parts of the city, an area which he'd formerly avoided. It also happened to be the posting stop for all the stage lines in and out of New York.

Cornwall frowned at the building. "But take a care. You don't want to be dragged into Burns's Rat Pit."

"Rat Pit?"

The doctor shivered through the heat. "Even worse, enticed up the stairs to far more despicable vices."

Matthew hesitated before the suddenly fascinating building.

"Get on with it, lad!"

He shook all sorts of questions from his head, leaving only the most pertinent one. "I'll need to know where we're going, sir."

Cornwall lowered his voice to a whisper directed at the boy's ear. "To Trenton, and thence to Princeton." He shifted his eyes warily around the bustling crowd of scruffy seamen and even less-reputable types. "No need to discuss details here. Never know who might be listening."

Matthew was confused. Confused by the occasion, the location, and the doctor's sudden suspicions. Most of all, he was confused by the destination. Princeton? What in the world could be waiting in Princeton?

"Not *what*, but *who*. Always who. In this instance, Aaron Burr." The doctor smiled. Twilight was closing in on them, and they were alone together at last, the only two occupants on the stage spur from Trenton to Princeton.

"It will be a test dig, as it were. The acquisition of an American original before we set sail for foreign climes." He rubbed his hands gleefully.

Matthew sat sweltering in his rolled up shirtsleeves opposite the doctor. The coach windows didn't open. They hadn't on the last stage, either. Just as well. Otherwise they would have been overcome by dust long before now. He stared fixedly through the grimy panes anyway, as he'd been doing all afternoon. He'd never been off Manhattan Island before in his life, and he did want to see the world. He cleared his throat of grit.

"I suppose you'll tell me who he is in good time."

"Burr?" Cornwall rearranged himself on the lumpy seat. "Therein lies a story, but I suppose we've leisure for it at the moment." He squinted through a window himself. "He started out at Princeton College, and ended up there, too. In between, he made quite a dashing figure as a young man, quite the ladies' man. He was a leading officer of the Revolution, always at loggerheads with General Washington, and after victory he rose quickly in the world of politics. Quickly enough to almost beat Jefferson in the presidential elections.

But almost wasn't good enough, and Burr ended up only vice president."

Matthew waited for the fall he knew must be coming. The objects of Cornwall's studies were usually flawed. "Was he—Burr—disappointed?"

The doctor chuckled. "Enraged might be a better description. It was mostly downhill from there. He got into an argument with Alexander Hamilton, another bigwig in our country's earlier days, and challenged him to a duel."

That piqued Matthew's interest. "What happened?"

"What happened was that he ended up shooting Hamilton, although some called it murder. Burr found himself *persona non grata*—" The doctor glanced at Matthew. "That's Latin, for nobody wanted to look him in the eye. He was cut from polite society."

Matthew only shrugged. Polite society meant nothing to him.

Cornwall noticed. "It can be fairly depressing when your best friends won't talk to you anymore, lad. In revenge, Burr took off for the West and got himself mixed up in another situation, one that some back East interpreted as treason against the government of the United States."

Night had fallen quite suddenly outside, as

suddenly as Aaron Burr's star, Matthew thought. He turned his head from the coach window. "It sounds as if this Burr was looking for trouble!"

"Could be. At any rate, it found him. He was dragged back East for a trial and was acquitted—"

"Like Henry Bedlow?"

Cornwall nodded. "Like Henry Bedlow. But no one believed Burr, either, so he exiled himself to Europe for a while. Eventually he came back home and tried to pick up the pieces. But by that time his wife and adored daughter were both dead, and Aaron Burr ended up wandering around New York City for years like the Ancient Mariner, just getting older and older." The doctor stopped. "Everyone knew who he was, but kept their distance. The man finally had the decency to die a few years back."

Matthew pinched a flea that had worked its way out of the upholstery. Then he scratched at its bite. "So why are you after Burr's head?"

"Why? Because he was brilliant, unique! Many's the time I shadowed him as he walked around the city, watching him attend the theater, attend places of less repute. But never quite getting close enough to that head of his. Never gathering the courage to accost him outright."

"You followed him? Dogged him, like a, a—"

Cornwall sighed. "Not like a predator, lad. It was sheer fascination. Even at eighty that man had charisma. He could have been president of the United States! He could have gone down in the history books! Instead, a flaw in his character changed everything. Don't you see? I need to know what it was in his makeup, in his skull, that precipitated all that!" The doctor held up his hands in supplication. "I need Aaron Burr's head for my book. Try to understand me, Matthew."

It was Matthew's turn to sigh. "I'm trying, sir. I truly am. But—"

"But what?"

"But why do you always choose imperfect men to study, sir?"

Cornwall smiled. "Who among us is perfect?"

"That's not what I mean, and I think you know it."

This time the doctor's sigh came from his very soul. "There's one little thing I left out when I told you about Mother Carey and her chickens. It's something I never confessed to anyone."

"You don't have to tell me, sir—"

"No. But I will. Maybe it will help to get it off my chest at last." Cornwall tapped his chest and a little puff of road dust rose from his shirt. He brushed at it, then raised his eyes to Matthew and revealed his secret.

"My own father was amongst that rioting mob, lad. My own *father*. I saw his face twisted with hatred and blood lust, heard him screaming for the gibbet for poor Bedlow. From that moment I took up books, true, but I also acquired a great fear of siring children of my own. What if I had inherited his madness? Even if it were only momentary? What if I brought children into the world like him?"

Cornwall's head jerked toward the blackness outside the window to hide the emotions running across his pudgy face, but he kept talking. "Ultimately, I seek practical applications from phrenology, Matthew. Why do I study flawed characters? From them someday I may find the solutions to reforming criminals, to treating the insane. From them—and from my studies of brilliant minds in Part Two—I hope to formulate a theory which will *scientifically alter* these negative propensities. I wish to do no less than find the solution to the perfecting of mankind!"

Matthew swallowed, suddenly speechless. He had been chosen to be a part of this Grand Plan! Wouldn't his own father, his own mother, be proud of their surviving son? But to be part of the Plan, he'd need to work hard to overcome his distaste of the methods, the grave robbing. It would take effort.

Outside the carriage, the post horses began to slow. They were entering the town of Princeton.

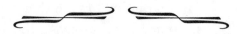

Matthew and Dr. Cornwall strolled around the town like two gentlemen of leisure the following day. Gripping his satchel in one hand, Cornwall pointed out the sights, which mostly consisted of the famous college. Slowly, casually, they were making their way toward Princeton Cemetery.

"Mustn't be too obvious about our mission, lad," the doctor murmured as he politely smiled and lifted his hat to a lady on the street. "To all intents and purposes I'm here to show off my *alma mater*, my old school, to my grandson, in the hopes that he might follow where I have led."

"Did you study at Princeton College, sir?"

Cornwall jammed the hat back on his head. "Don't be silly. Where would I have gotten the funds to attend a gentleman's school? I'm self-taught, and proud of it!"

"If you say so, sir." But Matthew noticed the covetous looks the doctor was still giving the impressive college buildings. "What about Aaron Burr?"

"Of course he attended here. His father and grandfather both were presidents of the college!"

"Oh, then—" But Matthew never got to finish his thought. Instead, he was knocked off his feet by a horse galloping past them as they crossed the street.

"Most inconsiderate!" Cornwall muttered as he reached his free hand down for the boy. "Could've done bodily damage!"

Matthew was flat on his bottom, staring at the disappearing rear end of the horse. "Did you see the rider, sir?"

"Only to notice that he was big, but I'd like to give him a piece of my mind!"

"Me, too!" Matthew struggled to his feet, dusting his trousers. "Well, let's at least get out of the street before someone else races by. Have we made enough of an impression yet to head for the cemetery? I'm feeling hungry and it would be nice to get the exploring over with before our dinner."

Brightening as always at the thought of food, Cornwall prodded Matthew forward. "An excellent suggestion. Then, perhaps, a little nap before the evening's exertions. From the innkeeper's directions the cemetery ought to be but a short walk ahead."

It was, and there amidst the bright green grass were rows of carefully spaced tombstones. Apparently there'd been a burial earlier in the day, for freshly turned dirt formed a new mound in the middle of a nearby row. Aside from a few grazing cows, the remainder of the cemetery was empty of living inhabitants. Matthew and the doctor continued the studied pacing of their stroll anyway, lingering over this stone or that in an effort at nonchalance. But Cornwall was having a hard time keeping up the charade.

"I can almost smell him, lad! There's a certain emanation in the air: frustrated dreams, hopes dashed, overweening pride thwarted. We're getting close!"

Matthew halted before a stone in the next row over. Slowly he read the inscription: "'Born February 5, 1756. Died September 14, 1836. A Colonel in the Army of the Revolution. Vice President of the United States from 1801 to 1805.' I've found him, sir!" Despite himself, he was excited. "I've found Aaron Burr!"

"Hush!" Cornwall quickly glanced around. "No reason to advertise our interest. Move on to the next stone."

Matthew moved, but there wasn't much point.

He'd barely vacated the space when the doctor began fondling the tombstone. He was cackling, too.

"Your hiding days are over, Burr. I've got you now! Your dark secrets will soon be in my hands!"

"Um, sir? Dr. Cornwall?" Matthew tugged at his employer. "You said we ought to be discreet. And there's a carriage starting through the gates—"

Cornwall sprang away from the stone, then turned back to run a hand over the incised double A's of "Aaron" once more. "Yes, yes, lad. Of course." He sighed and glanced up at the sun. "'Gallop apace, you fiery-footed steeds, and bring in cloudy night immediately!' I can hardly wait, Matthew."

Matthew had other thoughts about the night, and a few about his employer's sanity, too, Grand Plan or no. He kept his tongue on both those topics. "We've got the location, sir. How about some food?"

Cornwall calmed considerably during the course of a hearty meal. His stew bowl wiped clean, he finally rose, raising his voice for the innkeeper's benefit. "A rest during the heat of the afternoon might be called for, lad."

"Yes, sir." Matthew followed the doctor up the stairs. When the doctor fumbled with the key, he took over. "A little too much of the innkeeper's ale, sir. Allow me." He turned the key and pushed open the door. Then he just stood there.

"Forward, forward, my bed is waiting!" Cornwall pushed in behind him. He, too, stopped, dropping his satchel. "Really, this is too much. Too much."

In their absence, the room had been defiled. Bedcovers were strewn everywhere, and so were the contents of their luggage. Atop the mess sat Henry Bedlow. He was leering.

"My manuscript!" the doctor came alive at last. "Our war fund!"

Matthew collected himself sufficiently to turn to the doctor. "They both should be safe, sir. You've been carting them around in your satchel all morning."

"Oh." Cornwall snatched at his bag and clung to it. "So I have. So I have. Then all is not lost." He took a deep breath. "Nevertheless, this invasion is an outrage! Fetch the innkeeper, Master Morrissey. We must have a discussion at once!"

"Certainly, sir." But before descending the

stairs, Matthew carefully tucked Henry's cranium under a jumble of bedding. Not everyone appreciated the charm of skulls.

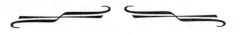

The innkeeper blinked at the chaos before him. "I'll have to charge you gentlemen extra for such a mess—"

"Don't be ridiculous, man." Cornwall was still upset. "We didn't make it!"

"Oh. Then mayhap I should send for the sheriff—"

Matthew cleared his throat. "Excuse me, but nothing seems to be stolen. We just need to know if anything unusual happened while we were out this morning. Anyone you didn't recognize—"

The innkeeper slowly rubbed at his chin. "There was this new feller come in for a drink or two. Poor horse was all lathered up—"

"And?" Cornwall prodded.

"What did he look like?" Matthew added.

The innkeeper was a slow thinker. He rubbed his chin some more. "The nature of my business, I get all sorts. Hard to keep 'em separate, but—"

"Yes?" Matthew and the doctor both asked.

"Well, he was a big feller. Real big. And seems

like, seems like he had this low, heavy brow. Kind of stood out, give him a mean sort of cast. Not his fault, I'm guessing. And then there was this scar. Mighty impressive. My good wife took note on it and refused to serve him. Retreated straight back to the kitchen, she did."

"What sort of a scar?" Matthew had an odd feeling building inside.

The innkeeper commenced scratching his head. "Strikes me it run clear down from his brow to his chin. He did favor the other side of his face. Seemed to favor solitude, too, so I give it to him. Went out back for a piece to tend his poor mount."

Cornwall rummaged in a pocket. He came up with a coin. "My thanks for your astute observational powers. We'll say no more about this incident. Just wanted you aware that we were not responsible for any damage."

The coin disappeared. "Sure enough, sure enough. You won't be needing Sheriff Walcott then?"

Cornwall pasted on a smile, but it was a little sickly. "Not at all. I'll just have my assistant here set things right."

The innkeeper nodded himself back down the stairs while Cornwall turned to Matthew. "Did you note something distinctive about that description, lad?"

That odd feeling centered itself in Matthew's stomach. "How many people could there be with low, jutting brows and such a scar? It sounded just like, just like"—he clutched at the burn—"the body snatcher from Potter's Field, sir. The body snatcher from the Fowlers' alley."

The doctor nodded. "Uncommonly like, I fear." He bent to open his satchel and retrieve his manuscript. "But my life's work is still with us, and our war—" He stopped to fumble madly in the bowels of his bag. "Our war funds. The money."

Matthew's stomach burn intensified. "What about the money, sir?"

"It comes back to me now. I thought the coins a tad heavy this morning, and rather than convey them on our stroll . . ."

"You didn't. You really didn't leave them in the room?" Matthew prayed that it wasn't so, even as he felt the enormity of the truth creep over him.

Cornwall merely crushed his manuscript to his chest and sank onto the bed.

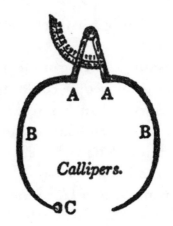

Callipers.

CHAPTER SEVEN

"SO NEAR, AND YET SO FAR . . ."

Dr. Cornwall perched on the foot of the high bed, his short legs dangling over the side, Henry Bedlow cradled in his lap. He was drumming his fingers against Henry's cranium. The motion stilled for a moment as he glanced past the lighted candlestick on the windowsill to the darkness beyond. "Considering recent events, dare we undertake the deed, or not?"

Matthew was gazing out the same window. It was darker here in the country than it ever got in New York City—a kind of pure blackness that he'd never encountered. Just yesterday morning he would have been overjoyed by the possibility of never entering a cemetery by night again. He would have been delighted to be free and clear of the grave-robbing side of the doctor's phrenology work. But the thought of that body snatcher following them, robbing them, trying to foil Dr. ABC's Grand Plan . . . *How* had the villain known they'd come to Princeton? *Why* had he pursued them? What was he really after? Not for a moment did Matthew believe that the stolen money was the principal purpose of the burglary. It was just an unexpected benefit. Think. *Who* could have sent him? . . . Was it the Fowlers? Cornwall's scholar and gentleman? Or a mysterious secret society? Then again, maybe the body snatcher had spied the doctor and himself in Potter's Field, followed them, and was working on his own agenda.

Matthew's whirling brain came up with no answers. Yet a certain resolve was building within him. He turned.

"We've come all this way, sir. I don't like the idea of someone trying to stop us."

"You don't like the idea? What about me?" Cornwall slapped Bedlow's skull. "The sheer impertinence of attempting to intimidate us, of trying to destroy our entire project by making off with our hard-earned funds! Where would science be if we let little events like that put a stop to our experimental studies? No, no—" The doctor dropped Henry onto the quilt and slipped to the floor. Before Matthew's eyes he straightened his stubby little figure. He became a man of destiny, a personage to contend with. "If one wishes to define the turning points of history as I do, to make an impact on the future—one must soldier on. Our mission is noble! These little skirmishes should only strengthen us."

"But without our traveling funds—"

Cornwall stiffened his resolve even further. "I've enough in my pocket to honorably settle accounts here at the inn, maybe even enough to get us back to New York to begin our fundraising again. In the meantime, nothing ventured, nothing gained. We'll worry about who's trying to thwart us later. For now, onward to Princeton Cemetery!"

Matthew gained heart with the return of the doctor's spirits. "Aye, aye, sir!" He shouldered the tool sack like a rifle and led the way.

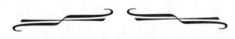

It was a night completely different from the April night spent in the fog of Potter's Field. The sky was a clean black dome broken only by the pin-pricks of a million stars. The air was soft, clear, and pure, disturbed only by a light, steady drone.

"Drat!" The doctor swung his satchel with one hand and slapped vigorously with the other. "I'd forgotten about Jersey mosquitoes!"

Matthew opened his mouth to answer, then found it invaded by the insects. He shifted his sack and did his own swatting. The remainder of the journey was accomplished in muffled silence.

Soon they were among the tombstones, counting off the rows and markers. Only a stone or two from their quarry, Cornwall gasped and clapped a hand to his heart. Matthew halted. "What is it, sir?"

The doctor was squinting at the cross. "This symbol!" he managed.

Matthew moved closer. "What symbol? It's just another marker, with a rose carved in the center of the cross."

"The symbol of the Rosicrucians!" Cornwall exclaimed. "A rose crucified upon a cross. And practically next to Aaron Burr!"

"Well, it's been next to him for some time now," Matthew pointed out.

"Of course, of course." The doctor pulled out a handkerchief to pat at his brow. "Just nerves after the events of the day."

They moved on to Aaron Burr. Matthew emptied the sack and stood poised with a tool.

"The same drill, sir?" he whispered. Cemeteries in the dark just seemed to bring on whispers. "Go for the top of the coffin?"

"Yes, get on with it. I can't imagine what further business that body snatcher could have here, tonight, so far from the medical students of New York, and with our money burning a hole in his pockets. Still—" He stopped and swiveled his head around. "Still, I keep expecting *something*."

Matthew spit on his hands, grabbed the pickax again, and swung its point earthward. As it struck, Cornwall shrieked out a single word:

"*Theodosia!*"

Matthew froze. "Now what?"

The doctor pointed a shaking finger into the distance. "Burr's beloved daughter. Drowned at sea. Coming out of that mausoleum!"

Matthew spun. There was something emerging from a nearby mausoleum. It was tall and slim and swathed in white billowing layers. Mouth ajar despite mosquitoes, Matthew watched as it danced closer. His spine felt like jelly. He leaned into the support of his pick, helpless to do anything else.

"Theodosia!" Cornwall cried out again.

"Forgive us! The desecration will cease and desist—"

Throaty laughter wafted toward them. "You've mistaken the lady, but still the effect is gratifying. Quite gratifying." The vision closed in. With but a row of tombstones distancing them it stilled its sinuous dance and made a deep curtsey. "Salome, darlings. Salome. Seeking the head of John the Baptist."

"What?" Cornwall choked out.

"Or if you prefer, Judith after the head of Holofernes. The precise identity is irrelevant. It's the head that is critical."

Matthew dropped his tool and sagged against the tombstone. "I don't understand."

"No, of course you don't." The figure lifted hands to its own head; seemed to detach it—

This time Matthew let out a screech.

More laughter as the hair was removed.

"A wig?" croaked Cornwall. He began swabbing himself with the handkerchief again. "I cannot comprehend—"

"Of course you can't." The wig was dropped and the figure moved closer. This time it bowed. "Peterson Preston-Smythe in performance, gentlemen. The next great tragedian, the next Edwin Forrest of our country. Presently a student at

Princeton College trying to obtain true realistic detail for the Drama Society's presentation of *Salome*." He twirled and his diaphanous skirts followed him. "Effective, no? I've been rehearsing the Dance of the Seven Veils, but I still need a *head*."

Matthew's jaw snapped shut. "You're an actor? Practicing in a cemetery in the middle of the night?"

"Rehearsing, my boy. The term is *rehearsing*."

Dr. Cornwall began to breathe freely again. He stuffed the handkerchief into his pocket with a vengeance. "What is it you want from us?"

"What would anyone hanging around a cemetery at night want? A body, of course." The actor paused. "Actually, just the head will do. I need to feel a real severed human head in my hands—if only for a few moments—in order to truly realize the inner essence of my role."

"Well, why don't you go and dig up your own?" snarled Cornwall, this culmination to the day's events further piercing his usual aplomb.

"Oh, I couldn't possibly soil my hands in such an endeavor. Against my principles. But I noted a fresh burial this morning, and had hoped that someone of your persuasion might—"

"We're not body snatchers!" Now Matthew was angry. "We're phrenologists seeking scientific specimens. And not fresh ones, either."

"Fresh, decayed, who cares?" Peterson Preston-Smythe indolently sank against a neighboring monument and carefully arranged his skirts. "I do happen to be on speaking terms with the local sheriff, however, and he might just be interested in grave-robbing *phrenologists—*"

The doctor threw up his hands. "Proceed with the chore, Matthew. This blackmailer shall have access to our find." He turned to the young man. "For fifteen minutes. Understood?"

Peterson Preston-Smythe smirked. "Understood."

"If that's what the students do, I don't think I want to go to Princeton College, either," Matthew remarked as he and the doctor trudged back to their accommodations under the lightening predawn sky.

Cornwall waved another cloud of mosquitoes from his path and stumbled on, a wilted figure. "It does give one pause, lad. Whither the scholarly world? What happened to the classics? Drama Society, humbug. And I wasn't totally convinced of that Preston-Smythe's sense of honor, either. I recommend we take the first affordable stage away from this place. Before we receive an unsolicited visit from the sheriff we've been hearing so much about."

"Or before someone else notices the rearrangement of the turf over Aaron Burr's coffin," Matthew added.

Cornwall sighed. "That too. That too." He swung the satchel and brightened marginally. "Not a totally satisfactory day, but we have got our specimen. I just hope Burr will forgive me the final ignominy of being waltzed around the cemetery in the arms of that, that *purveyor of sensationalism.*"

The first affordable coach went to Philadelphia. Matthew and the doctor went with it. Exhausted by their recent labors and the specter of abject poverty—not to mention hunger pangs—they both dozed until they found themselves surrounded by their luggage on the dusty street of another new place.

"What do we do next, sir?" Matthew sank atop a bag and studied colorfully painted brick houses surrounding them on one side, a bustling market arcade on the other.

"I suppose we search out an inn."

"With what money?" Matthew asked. "We

haven't even enough to buy a bowl of porridge."

Cornwall ignored the obvious. "After we've rested up, I'd dearly love to examine our prize. Then we can begin planning—"

"La!" The shriek came from under the arches of the market across the street. It repeated itself, growing in intensity as it closed in on them. "La! It couldn't be. But it is! Dr. Cornwall himself!"

Asa B. Cornwall's look of bemusement turned from dawning recognition, to panic, to new-found hope. "Elsie, er, Mrs. Higginbotham! What a rare surprise!"

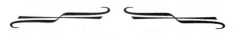

"Imagine you coming all the way to Philadelphia and not looking me up." Mrs. Higginbotham swung a basket laden with fresh berries onto the stoop of a prominent house several blocks from the market. She yanked the bellpull. "My daughter has all the room in the world. Besides, there isn't a decent phrenologist in the entire city, and she and her husband both need to be read."

Matthew stood by the doctor's luggage wondering if—even with starvation threatening them—Elsie Higginbotham was the best solution to their current problem. He was also wondering what might happen next when a liveried servant grandly opened the door. Hovering behind the servant was a younger, slightly less copious version of Elsie Higginbotham.

"My daughter Felicity," burbled Mrs. Higginbotham. "Let us in, darling. I've brought us strawberries and guests, both!"

Matthew followed another servant up a spiral staircase to a bedroom. He loosened his tensed arms enough to drop the luggage as Mrs. Higginbotham warbled up the stairs.

"Master Morrissey? Freshen up later, dearie. You're needed down here for your usual assistance. The good doctor has agreed to begin immediately!"

Relieved at having something to do, Matthew rooted in the nearest satchel for the doctor's calipers. Bearing the instrument before him, he decorously descended the stairs.

Dr. Cornwall was waiting in the parlor, focused on Mrs. Higginbotham's daughter. "Ah, then, Madam Felicity. A most felicitous name, if I might say so." He was rewarded with a giggle and barely managed to disguise his wince. "Let us see if it is deserving. The calipers, please, Master Morrissey."

"*Mais, oui.*" Matthew strode into service.

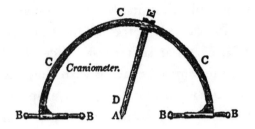

Craniometer.

CHAPTER EIGHT

"Might I have a word with you, sir?"

Matthew stood in the doorway of the adjoining guest room, watching Cornwall struggle out of his shoes. They'd been in Philadelphia for an entire week. The doctor had been busy with a seemingly endless stream of new clients procured under the patronage of Mrs. Higginbotham and her daughter. Matthew had had time for little but to stand by in the formal parlor practicing his French, or handing the doctor his phrenological implements.

Filling the space between patients were meals.

Countless meals with endless delicacies presented by almost invisible servants. Matthew felt as though he and the doctor were being fattened up for some ritual sacrifice. What sort of sacrifice, he wasn't sure. But he fervently began to wish that the heathen hordes for whom he used to give up his pennies at church would come and finish them off quickly. Being boiled in a great cauldron would be preferable to having to spend any more time whatsoever in the vicinity of all these gushing females. True, there were only two of them, but somehow Elsie and Felicity seemed like more. Much more.

Matthew cleared his throat and tried his question again. "A word, sir?" The doctor finally acknowledged him.

"It's late, lad, and I feel unaccountably exhausted."

Matthew pushed shut the door behind him anyway. "Of course you're exhausted. Between all the analyses you've done, and all the food you've eaten—"

Cornwall rubbed his distended stomach. "But such food! That veal in marsala tonight, and the Baked Alaska. . . It's almost worth the indigestion." He burped. "And we even made the local papers! Were you listening to Elsie read out that piece about us between courses?"

"It was about you, sir. And it only said that 'the eminent New York phrenologist, Dr. Asa B. Cornwall, is currently a guest at the home of Lucas Whitticome, Esquire, and his wife, notable in charitable circles in our city.' Society news, sir."

"But free advertisement nevertheless."

"Is that what you're after? What about Aaron Burr, sir? Have you even studied him yet?"

"Of course I've studied him!" Cornwall grabbed for his stomach again. "At least sufficiently to find that his organs of Secretiveness and Destructiveness were greatly enlarged—"

"The obvious," Matthew stated. "I could have made that analysis."

Cornwall didn't take the bait. "Burr has waited this long for my attentions. I suspect he won't mind waiting a little longer for a more extensive examination."

Matthew threw out his arms. "What about your Grand Plan? What about Part Two? Or are we to be stranded in Philadelphia forever? Reading *society* heads."

"Ah, to be young again," Cornwall mumbled as he slipped off his neck scarf and loosened the collar of his shirt. "When a week went on indefinitely. When immediate action was everything." He struggled with his jacket. "Help me out of this, lad."

Matthew stepped closer to tug at a sleeve. "Another week of this food and you'll have to order another new wardrobe, sir."

"Another week in Philadelphia and I'll be able to afford it." He winked at Matthew. "We're getting our old, full prices here, Matthew, and twice as many patients, even if they are rather boring society heads. Elsie's daughter has been most gracious in her support of our endeavor. As has Elsie herself, of course—" Cornwall writhed from his jacket. "Have a little patience."

Matthew was running out of patience. "I know we've got to build our war fund again, but isn't there any other way?"

"What else can I do, boy?" The doctor's own voice turned frustrated. "Marry Elsie so we can use her money to go abroad?"

Maybe *that* was the ritual sacrifice for which they were being fattened. Matthew draped the jacket over a waiting chair. "Not if Elsie has to go with us."

"I was joking!" Dr. Cornwall stroked the strands of hair crossing his head. "Still. Marriage . . . with Elsie, yet *without* Elsie . . ." He plopped against his pillows. "Bring me Henry Bedlow. I need some inspiration."

Matthew was appalled by the results of his conversation with Dr. Cornwall. Instead of blithely ignoring Elsie Higginbotham's ludicrous advances, his master was now playing to them. Meanwhile, their consultation fees piled up, but even Matthew began to understand that the money might never be enough for the extended excursion to foreign shores that the doctor planned.

In growing desperation Matthew tended to their clients, settling them onto the Empire couch, spreading the drapery of the windows as wide as possible to catch the best light, standing by with calipers and craniometer—now on a gleaming silver tray. Asa B. Cornwall's small talk with the patients went through one ear and out the other. Until the afternoon a quite elegant older woman was ushered into the parlor and presented by the butler.

"Mrs. Elizabeth Mordecai to see the doctor."

Cornwall made his little bow. "Madam Mordecai—" Then he paused and really looked at the woman. "You wouldn't be related to the brilliant financier Nicholas Mordecai, by any chance?"

Mrs. Mordecai removed her flower-sprigged bonnet, revealing neatly waved gray hair, then eased onto the couch and settled her large, flouncy sleeves. "How kind of you to remember my late husband, Dr. Cornwall."

"But, madam, his renown was universal. It's said he was the inspiration behind Alexander Hamilton, that he single-handedly set our country's finances aright after the debacle of the War of 1812. . . ." Cornwall paused and stretched out a hand. Matthew deposited the calipers in them. "But I had thought he passed away overseas."

"In Paris," she calmly answered. "I brought him home to Philadelphia so I could be near him."

"Most admirable."

Cornwall began humming to himself as he examined the venerable gray head with gentle vigor. Matthew felt goose bumps rising on his arms. That humming. It meant the doctor was thinking. About something besides either Elsie or food. Instead of feeling relief, his instant reaction was, *Heaven help us both, the man is plotting again.*

At supper that evening Asa B. Cornwall ate his usual three dozen oysters. Next he consumed his consommé. When the roast beef was presented he accepted a single slice. He refused all further offerings.

"Asa, dear?" Elsie Higginbotham gazed upon the object of her affection with growing concern. "Are you quite well?"

"Tip-top, Elsie. But I feel the need for some evening air, and fear I couldn't manage a walk if I succumbed to my usual helpings of your bounteous table."

A dish of creamed something or other was wafted before Mrs. Higginbotham's nose. Matthew watched with interest as the usual gluttonous pleasure crossed her face. Then her small eyes tightened and she pushed the platter away. "Nothing else for me, either. A walk sounds lovely."

Matthew shot his eyes toward the doctor, saw him nervously sip at his wine. "I had in mind quite a long walk, my dear."

Mrs. Higginbotham shoved her bulk from her chair. "The longer the better." Then her determination faltered. "You'll save some dessert for us, Felicity?"

Felicity was beaming knowingly at her eversilent husband. "Of course, Mama. Shall I fetch your bonnet for you?"

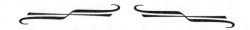

Matthew waited up for the doctor's return. When he heard the heavy steps cross the hallway, heard the neighboring door firmly close, he popped through the adjoining entry.

"What's going on, sir?"

Cornwall was hanging on to his bedpost, red-faced and puffing. "What's going on is that that dreadful woman attacked me. And she was nearly victorious. *Tentacles*," he yelped. "Like an *octopus!*" He sank onto the mattress. "I merely wanted to have a little walk, preferably in your company. A little exploratory walk to confirm the location of a certain final resting place. At least that much was accomplished." He kicked his legs. "I can't do it, Matthew. I simply can't!"

"Can't what, sir?"

"I can't marry Elsie for her money. I've tried to justify it a thousand different ways, but the end result is always the same: Elsie Higginbotham!"

"Lower your voice, sir," Matthew warned as he knelt to pull off the doctor's shoes. At the moment his master needed all the help he could get.

Cornwall caught the boy's shoulders in a death grip as his voice ground down to a harsh whisper.

"I can't! I can't! I can't! If I could get past Elsie herself, I'd still be stuck with this humiliating lifestyle. You were right. I'm turning into a society entertainment, Matthew!" A wail of despair followed. "I'm a serious scientist, not some Gypsy palmist!"

Matthew silently managed the shoes, then finally spoke. "I knew the truth would come to you eventually. We'll find the rest of the money somewhere. We can go back to New York and work at our own pace, like before. When do you want me to pack our bags?"

The grip loosened. "Not so fast. We have a bit of real business to deal with before we make our farewells to Philadelphia."

Matthew raised his head to meet Cornwall's eyes. The listlessness of the past weeks was gone from them. They were bright and sharp again. He knew the meaning of that look.

"But nobody truly important is buried in Philadelphia, sir. Except for Benjamin Franklin. And you wouldn't really . . . No. You couldn't be considering him. It would be sacrilege!"

The doctor smiled. "For once I agree with you, lad. It would be akin to going after George Washington or even Thomas Jefferson. No, we won't disturb Ben Franklin. But I do believe I deserve a souvenir of our sojourn in this city. And who was to guess that one of the most brilliant of financial minds was lodged here? Not eight blocks from this very room!"

Matthew sighed, but with relief. Thank goodness that elegant old lady had come for a reading this afternoon. Thank goodness she'd woken his master from his sleep. Matthew would be very certain to approach her husband's grave carefully. He'd make very certain to leave no signs to distress the woman. "Nicholas Mordecai?"

"Ah, Matthew, Matthew." Cornwall patted the boy's head fondly. "Perceptive as always. I'm not certain at all how I got along without you all these years." He kicked the shoes under his bed. "But not tonight. Possibly not even tomorrow night. I'm afraid I'm going to have to watch my diet for a few days. Try to recapture my old form and energy."

"Porridge it is, then, sir." Matthew grinned. "A small bowl, three meals only. I'll just leave the order with the cook before I head for my own bed."

Cornwall flopped onto the counterpane. "Snuff the candle as you leave, lad."

CHAPTER NINE

Matthew had the bags packed. He'd hidden them in the butler's pantry and carefully unbolted the rear door of Felicity's home so he and the doctor could make a quick exit into the night after their cemetery chores were done. Yes, they would be absconding without good-byes, but they'd be stealing none of the silver, stealing nothing but Elsie Higginbotham's heart. And Matthew was quite certain that a few good meals would quickly ease Elsie's pain.

He made a last-minute survey of his room to be sure he'd forgotten nothing. Then he checked his person. The money belt beneath his shirt felt unusual, but not uncomfortable. The doctor was wearing a similar one. They'd not be fleeced twice. Matthew picked up the candlestick and walked into Cornwall's room.

"Is your manuscript packed, sir?"

The doctor was bending over his satchel. "Right here, lad. With plenty of room still for an extra head or two!" He snapped it shut, straightened to pat the money-belt bulge that blended into his paunch, and smiled. "Amazing how frisky these little night jaunts make me feel. Sometimes I think it's more than just anticipating a new specimen that does it. Maybe it's the sense of *adventure*."

For himself, Matthew guessed it was more a sense of fear. He wasn't overjoyed by the thought of going after Nicholas Mordecai, but tonight he was delighted to be escaping Elsie and her daughter. "Did you finish your thank-you letter, sir?"

"Yes, yes." Cornwall pointed to a sheet of paper lying on his pillow. "I do hate bread-and-butter notes as much as I hate the subterfuge, but I suppose it's all necessary. I realize that Elsie wouldn't let me out of her grasp face-to-face, or any other way." He studied the room a final time. Outside, a bell tower struck half past one. "Well, then, onward and upward, lad. Or should that be downward?"

Matthew pointed to the floor. "For starters. Slip off your shoes, sir. We'll have to do the steps in our stocking feet."

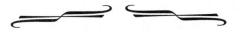

The night was different yet again from their other cemetery excursions. Clouds scudded across a haloed half moon, and the air had a thick heaviness to it.

"Rain tomorrow," Cornwall observed. He picked up his pace.

Matthew trotted behind with the tool sack till they reached the graveyard wall. This one was brick, and low. They clambered over it with ease and entered the path between a row of ornamented family vaults.

"You're sure Mordecai isn't in one of these, sir?" Matthew asked. "You'd think, as rich as he was—"

"Apparently he was also modest, lad. Either that, or his good widow conceived of better uses for the money." Cornwall broke past the dark alley of opulent tombs, then paused. "There he is, third stone over."

Matthew pulled out his shovel. He'd diligently

planned the night's procedure. First, he would cut perfect squares of turf that could be neatly set back after the grave dirt had been repacked. When he burrowed for the coffin, he'd be careful not to scatter the soil. He spread a blanket he'd brought for the purpose. Just pile the dirt upon it, shake the last, telling clods of soil atop the packed earth after the excavation was completed, then top it all off with the turf. The burial site would look nearly untouched. *If it's worth doing, it's worth doing well.* His father's favorite saying ran through his head, in his father's voice. John Morrissey might not be pleased by this part of the profession his son had found for himself, but he would be proud that Matthew was taking pains with the labor.

Matthew raised his eyes to the sky. In a moment, another dark bank of clouds would be hiding the moon's light. Yes, here it came. He slid from the shadows and began.

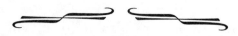

"Do you have a match, sir?"

Matthew's shovel had just struck a hard surface. It felt different from the usual wood, though. Cornwall bent down and offered the light.

"What have we got here?"

"I'm not sure." Matthew tapped the coffin again. "Lead, perhaps?"

"Blast. We have no cutters. How will we get inside?"

Matthew stretched his aching shoulders. "Maybe I could break through with the pick, then peel it up in layers?"

The flame of the match head caught Cornwall's fingers. He gave a little *yip* and dropped it. "It's too late to go in search of other tools, but we'll remember in the future. Cutters."

"A crowbar, too," Matthew added. "Hand me the pick."

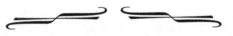

The lead was thinner than Matthew had expected, barely more than an eighth of an inch. Luckily, it hadn't been soldered closed, only layered atop the wood. Still, his fingers were cut and bloodied from the effort of bending back the jagged edges of the soft metal before he was staring at the coffin again in the light of the reappearing moon. "Here's the next surface," he called up. He touched it. "Hardwood, not soft pine."

"Get a move on, lad. The night is waning."

Matthew hefted the pickax again, struck several times, then stumbled back from an unexpected gleam. "I need another match!"

Cornwall stuck his head in the hole. "What is it now?"

"I'm not sure. The inner coffin seems to be lined with something bright—"

The fresh match was lowered.

"Gold!" Cornwall exclaimed.

"Coins!" Matthew breathed. "Poured all over Mordecai's chest!" He used the pick's prong to enlarge the opening. "With more pillowing his head!"

"You *can* take it with you!" the doctor chortled with glee. Then he was in the pit, too.

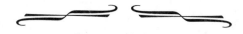

The satchel wasn't large enough for Mordecai and his money. Matthew stuffed the tool sack with the excess coins after he decided he'd have to discreetly abandon the tools. Then there was the chore of refilling the grave, stamping the fresh mound flat, rearranging the jigsaw puzzle of turf under an ominously lightening sky. At last Matthew ran his hands over the blades of grass, smoothing out footprints. Cornwall was tugging at him by this time.

"For goodness' sake, lad. The faculty of Conscientiousness can be overdone. We've got to get out of here! Dawn is almost upon us!

We've got to fetch our luggage before it's too late!"

Matthew rose from the ground and brushed the dirt from his knees. "It's probably already too late, sir. And now that we've a new war fund—" The sheer *size* of the new war fund stopped his tongue for a moment. It was enough to addle anyone. He took a deep breath and tried again. "Wouldn't it be better to leave the luggage? Cut our losses before we're caught? Just make our way to the waterfront and catch the first ship sailing for Europe?"

Cornwall was already half-carrying, half-dragging his heavily burdened satchel toward the cemetery wall. "You want me to desert Aaron Burr? Leave Henry Bedlow behind? Before even proving their usefulness? Never!"

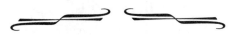

Matthew stashed Dr. Cornwall and their new war fund behind the backyard privy and raced toward the kitchen. The sky had lightened only so far, then settled into a gray murk. Rain began to fall.

"Good," Matthew murmured to himself. Rain made people sleepy. Maybe Felicity's cook and kitchen girl would lie in their beds a little longer this morning. He reached for the unlocked door and darted his head inside. The hearth was still cold. Two bags. He'd just have to fetch two bags. He crossed the threshold and bolted for the pantry; unfastened a cupboard and bent to reach in—

The swinging door behind crashed open, nearly crushing him into the corner.

"Lordy," a voice complained. "That old bed didn't want to let go of me this morning."

"Wish we could sleep late, the way some folks do around here," another voice whined.

"After you've made your fortune washing dishes, Missy Rachel, you can sleep late, too. In the meanwhile get that fire started!"

A sigh. "Yes, Cook."

At last the two women were through the passageway and Matthew was unfolding himself. What to do? Could he still make his escape through the kitchen? Blast the doctor's precious heads! Then a thought came to him. He pulled out the satchels. Next he reached for the neat stack of table linens sitting on a shelf behind. He chose a knife from the rack waiting above the counter and performed a little surgery on the cloth. Finally he rummaged in a bag for Henry Bedlow.

In a moment he had the tablecloth pulled over his damp hair, with Bedlow lodged atop his head.

Matthew fumbled for the two bags and pulled them under the tent of cloth. Staring through the eyeholes he'd made, he stumbled into the kitchen, moaning for all he was worth.

"*Ooooooooooh . . .*"

"Is that you back from the privy already, Cook? The bowels a little off this morning, are they?" The scullery maid looked up from the fire she was laying, then let out a piercing scream. Matthew lumbered past her, still moaning, straight into the backyard. The privy door shot open and Cook poked her head out. "You go and burn yourself again, Rachel?" Then *she* began screaming. Mercifully, she also shut and bolted the privy door.

Matthew made it to the rear of the shack and bounced Henry into his arms.

"What took you so long?" grumbled Cornwall under his breath. He glanced again at Matthew. "Didn't I tell you Bedlow could be useful?"

"We wouldn't have needed him if we hadn't come back!" Matthew tore off the cloth. "And he'll be totally wasted," he hissed, "if we don't get out of here *now*. Those screams probably woke even Elsie!"

Their weighty burdens didn't keep them in the yard a moment longer.

CHAPTER TEN

"TWO HUNDRED AND EIGHT, TWO HUNDRED AND nine, two hundred and ten . . ." The coins clinked atop their fellows, a growing pile of incredible brightness in the dimness of the ship's cabin. On his knees by the chest, Matthew paused on the two hundred and eleventh to study it more closely. "All of them the same," he murmured wonderingly. "All with this wonderful eagle."

"Yes, it is a splendid bird, isn't it?" Dr. Cornwall sat on the edge of the lower bunk, pen in hand and a tally sheet spread across his knees. "That's why they call these coins *eagles*." He plucked at the coin serving as a paperweight. "The Goddess of Liberty on the reverse isn't too shabby, either. Definitely my kind of woman." Cornwall hummed a few short notes of celebratory joy. "These ten-dollar gold pieces were all minted back in 1804. It seems that Mordecai cornered and held on to a larger hunk than the Bank of the United States itself."

Matthew's eyes were riveted on the gleaming pile. "It's an awful amount of money, isn't it sir?"

"Indeed. It puts me in absolute awe."

"But it's a little scary, too."

Cornwall grinned. "Keep counting, Master Morrissey, so we can learn exactly how scared we need to be."

Matthew tossed the two hundred and eleventh ten-dollar gold piece into the trunk and reached his hand into the tool sack for another fistful. "Two hundred and twelve, two hundred and thirteen, two hundred and fourteen . . ."

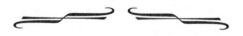

The *Fair Florinda* sailed down the Delaware River to the sea in a rainy dusk. Earlier, Matthew had stood on the deck as the ship was being piloted from its dock. *We made it*, he congratulated himself. *We've actually succeeded!* After the backyard escape they'd found a carriage to convey them and their bags to a riverfront lodging place. Once there, Matthew had stood watch over their belongings while the doctor went in search of a ship—any ship—leaving the port of Philadelphia the soonest. He'd returned delighted with the news that he'd secured passage for them to England, sailing that very evening. Next it was Matthew's turn to explore the shops for a suitable trunk for their war fund, and to run after bits of this and that which Cornwall had suddenly decided they couldn't live without now that they had the means.

Matthew gazed at the shore a final time. He was saying good-bye to Philadelphia and to the entire United States of America. Saying good-bye to his family buried somewhere in New York City. Even making silent farewells to Elsie and Felicity. There was no one else he really knew to send good-byes to. For better or worse he'd cast his lot with Dr. Asa B. Cornwall. The doctor's future was his future. No one else—

Matthew found himself squinting hard through the drizzle at the crowd of sailors, well-wishers, and wharf rats who crowded the receding dock.

It couldn't be.

No. Just his imagination acting up. He shook his head to clear it. For a moment there, just a brief moment, he thought he'd caught sight of a face with a jutting brow; a face with a long, jagged scar. He turned abruptly and clambered down the companionway to the waiting cabin.

"Five hundred and sixty-eight, five hundred and sixty-nine—" The body snatcher's image invaded Matthew's mind again. "Five hundred and seventy. Sir?"

Cornwall glanced up from his columns of figures. "We've emptied the sack? I thought there'd be a few more—"

"No, no, there are lots of coins left." Matthew hefted the sack in proof, then tossed it jangling back to the cabin floor. "A curious thing happened when we were casting off. I meant to say something about it, but—"

Cornwall jabbed his pen tip into the inkwell precariously balanced next to him atop the bunk. "If it happened on the dock it's now ancient history, lad. We've cut our ties, bolted from the barn. There's nothing back there that can affect us now!"

"Not even the body snatcher?"

"*What!*"

Cornwall nearly knocked over the inkwell. Matthew lunged for it and set it upon the floor, then caught his breath again. "That was my feeling, sir. It seemed unbelievable. Too, too—"

"Coincidental," the doctor stated. "Has he been following us since Princeton? And how could he have found us, lodged as we were with Elsie?"

"We weren't exactly hiding our presence, sir."

"I suppose not." Cornwall scratched absently at his head with the nib of his pen, leaving a streak of black ink across his pate. "Then there was that notice in the newspaper. But I hadn't thought our resurrectionist acquaintance would be literate enough to . . ."

"Me neither, sir. He hardly looks like he'd be able to talk."

"It all comes back to brains, lad, to the head," Cornwall thought aloud. "As I said back in New York, we're looking for a larger mind."

The floor beneath his feet suddenly canted and Matthew slipped down to it, then grabbed for the sliding inkwell. This time he securely replaced the stopper. "I haven't forgotten, sir.

But none of our suspects makes sense."

"Grave digging . . . medicine . . . no, phrenology . . . It has to be!"

"What has to be?" Matthew asked.

"Not what, but *who* again. Perhaps you were correct all along about those Fowler brothers of yours. About their being annoyed by my giving them a little competition."

"Maybe back in New York, but we've been away for weeks now."

"True." Cornwall set down his pen. Then he brightened. "But you mentioned they were sending apprentices out on the road. Could they consider the entire United States their exclusive phrenological domain?"

Matthew leaned against the wall of the cabin. He listened to the sound of waves slapping against the hull as he tried to remember exactly what Orson Squire Fowler had been like. Biggish. The unbecoming, overlong beard. The sharp, too bright teeth. The zealousness with which the man had given him an incorrect analysis. He finally shrugged. "I don't know. The Fowler I met seemed like a fairly ordinary, enthusiastic businessman."

Cornwall threw up his hands. "It's all water over the dam anyhow. We've left the Fowlers the entire territory. I believe we can stop worrying about body snatchers and burglars. Except in regard to our little war chest here." He picked up his pen again, smiling with renewed anticipation. "And we have still to learn the full depths of Nicholas Mordecai's posthumous bequest to us."

Matthew hauled himself over to the sack and proceeded with the count.

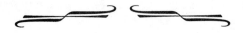

One thousand, seven hundred and twenty-seven ten-dollar gold pieces. Mordecai had given them more than seventeen thousand dollars! In the course of the next six weeks of their journey across the ocean, Matthew considered the impossible sum in his head again and again. It was a fair crossing, and he did most of his considering standing in the prow of the ship with the cool wind blowing his hair, the sails billowing above him. He watched for dolphins and whales, or just admired the changing colors of the sea and sky.

Asa B. Cornwall and he, Matthew Morrissey, were rich. How rich, he couldn't quite fathom, so he'd asked the doctor.

"Exactly how rich are we, sir?"

Cornwall beamed. "Look at it this way, lad. I've heard that the entire government of the

United States of America is run for a full year on little more than twice this amount."

Matthew whistled. "The entire United States, including the territories?"

The doctor nodded.

"That's rich."

Only then, perhaps a little belatedly, did Matthew think about the morality of their actions. Did emptying the coffin make them thieves? His mother wouldn't be happy to think of her son as a thief. She'd been kind, but rock solid in her beliefs about right and wrong, and he'd been spanked more than once—with tears on both sides—until she'd drummed the same beliefs into him. Matthew ran that thought past the doctor, too.

"Thieves! Don't be silly, boy. It was found money. Buried treasure. We didn't go looking for it, and we didn't steal it from Mordecai's home or his widow. It was just lying there, in the course of our scientific excavations. It would have been ridiculous to leave it."

Matthew eventually granted the reasonableness of Cornwall's stand. Besides, he couldn't see how all that money was going to ever help what was left of Mordecai in his grave.

It hadn't seemed to change the doctor much, either. Some people, confronted with such wealth, might abandon their life's work for pleasure. But the doctor hadn't an ounce of sloth or greed in his body. For him, the money was only a means to his goal. Something to grease the wheels of his efforts, make it all a little easier. Since they'd found the treasure and taken passage, the doctor was all business again. He spent hours in their little cabin studying Burr and Mordecai, scribbling lavish notes for his manuscript. He just came up on deck for air a few times a day. Otherwise, Matthew only saw him at the captain's table for meals, or during the daily three hours the doctor had decreed were necessary for overseeing Matthew's education.

Cornwall wasn't fooling around with these studies, either. He'd devised an entire program for Matthew. There was an hour of French. That was followed by an hour of history. Not surprisingly, the doctor looked at history from the point of view of leaders, men he called *pivots*, or *fulcrums*. Men who, because of their actions, had changed the world. Matthew was becoming quite familiar with the military exploits of Darius, Alexander the Great, Julius Caesar, Tamerlane, William the Conqueror, Charlemagne—and, of course, Napoleon. The last study hour was divided between mathematical and physiological subjects.

Then he was free to roam the ship for a few hours. But he was still expected to devote more private time to his studies in the course of each day.

Matthew didn't mind. The more he read, the more he could almost feel his brain beginning to grow. Beginning to expand. He wasn't sure he wanted to end up exactly like Dr. Cornwall, but he did know that he enjoyed learning things. That and the sea air were enough for now. There'd be time for worrying over his future later.

"Ugh!" Matthew tugged at the war chest. He bent over, grabbed a leather handle, and tried again. "I know we've got to keep this trunk in our own hands, and I'm not complaining, but what do you suppose it weighs?"

Cornwall turned from the tiny cabin porthole and its view of the docks and city of London. The *Fair Florinda* had already cast her anchor in the River Thames. It was time to disembark. "Sixty-six point six pounds, lad," the doctor cheerfully replied. He began stuffing skulls into a satchel. "Not counting the weight of the chest itself, of course."

Matthew, dumbfounded, managed to hoist the

chest waist-high. "How did you come up with that?"

"Mathematics, lad. Mathematics. If one happens to know that each coin weighs in at precisely 17.5 grams, and one also happens to know that 453.59 grams equals a pound, then all you need do is—"

"Multiply 17.5 times the number of coins, then divide by 453.59," Matthew finished.

"Exactly!" Cornwall beamed.

"And each coin we spend will make the load 17.5 grams lighter." Matthew staggered toward the door. "Doctor, sir, I think it's time we spent some money."

CHAPTER ELEVEN

LONDON WAS OLDER AND BIGGER AND TEEMING WITH even more life than New York. Matthew and Dr. Cornwall moved into a plush hotel, consigned their war chest to its vault, and set about exploring.

"As we're here, we might as well take in the sights, lad," the doctor had declared. "We'll give ourselves a few weeks to recover from the sea journey before we take on the Continent."

"That's fine with me, sir," Matthew answered. And it was. Who wouldn't enjoy the luxury of taking carriages after a lifetime of walking? Who wouldn't enjoy strolling into a fine jeweler's shop with the doctor and being allowed to choose a gold watch and fob to dangle from the pockets of one's new waistcoat? To have boots specially cobbled from the most supple leather to replace the tight and shabby old ones? To be barbered and supped like royalty?

But after he was thoroughly polished and stuffed to the gills, Matthew became restless. Not even the secret thrill of wandering through the great cathedral of Westminster Abbey and realizing that it was entirely too public a place for Dr. Cornwall to ever get his clutches on the famous remains buried *there* was sufficient. The doctor did wring his hands over the tantalizing proximity of luminaries such as Sir Isaac Newton and the poets Spenser and Dryden, but luckily was diverted by discovering the British Museum. Thereafter he was delighted to spend his days at the museum furthering his research. Matthew could only admire the Elgin Marbles, the Rosetta Stone, and bits of Egyptian papyrus for so long. Finally, it was enough.

"Enough? How could it ever be enough?" Cornwall asked him one evening in their rooms.

Matthew jiggled from foot to foot. "I'm used

to *doing* things, sir. I *need* to do something."

Cornwall tugged at a strand of hair. "Hum. We'll be crossing the Channel soon, and there'll be plenty for you to do in France. . . . But I do need a few more weeks for my studies. Can't have you getting into mischief in the meantime, though, can we? Well, you've got pocket money. Browse in the bookshops."

"Bookshops!" Matthew grumbled to himself. That would be the doctor's answer to everything. But the next morning he did browse in the bookshops, and made a startling discovery. There existed more than just grammars and dense tomes of science and history. There existed something called *fiction*.

Fiction was make-believe stories, and they were wonderful. As a dank, rainy autumn settled over London, Matthew curled up by the fire in his room with a pot of tea and a plate of cakes by his side. He galloped through *Ivanhoe* and *Rob Roy* and *Oliver Twist*, reading till his head was swimming. He went out only to haul back more piles of magazines, serialized stories, and novels. Then one day he found *Frankenstein*.

Frankenstein was different. It had strange places and stranger people. But it was also about science, the sort of science that pushed limits, the way Dr. Cornwall and phrenology did. Knowing the doctor so well, Matthew completely understood Dr. Frankenstein's passion for research, his passion to create something extraordinary. Matthew found himself biting his fingernails to the quick, visualizing Frankenstein's visits to charnel houses . . . so like Matthew's own dark night visits to cemeteries. Imagining the scientist's collection of bones. He understood the compulsion, and was scared silly by its results.

Victor Frankenstein's monster set Matthew's skin creeping. The creature was so familiar that the obvious connection took a while to dawn on him. When it did, it was the middle of the night, in a dream. Clearly, so clearly he saw the lumbering monster. He saw his scraggly hair falling over his shoulders. Saw the long jagged scar as the creature presented his half profile. Smelled the smell of the graveyard pulsing from him. When Frankenstein's monster turned full face, holding out a hand in supplication, Matthew woke up screaming.

"The body snatcher! The body snatcher!"

Trembling, Matthew rose to try to light a lamp. His fingers shook so that he wasted three matches until one burst into fire. He studied the flame carefully before he got the lamp going. Then he

132

picked up the light and carried it to the mirror sitting atop his dressing table. Still shaking, he set down the lamp and studied his image. His face was strained, his hair tousled from uneasy sleep. How could his sleep have been anything but uneasy? For when the monster had turned, it was his own face he'd seen.

He, Matthew Morrissey, was the monster.

Matthew stifled a sob as the door to the adjoining room opened. Dr. Cornwall hurried over in his rumpled nightshirt, blinking like an owl.

"What is it, lad? Another dream?"

Matthew gulped back tears. "A nightmare, sir. In it, I was . . . I was the *body snatcher!*"

Cornwall awkwardly patted his assistant's shoulders. "Stuff and nonsense, my boy. Stuff and nonsense. I didn't think it possible, but perhaps you've been doing too much reading. Maybe it's time we took to the road again. Fresh pastures, that's what you need."

Matthew rubbed a sleeve across his nose and swallowed twice. He wasn't convinced. Wasn't certain the doctor wasn't turning *him* into the one thing he most loathed and feared.

It seemed the doctor read his mind. "You're too decent a young man to ever sink to that level, and the help you've been giving me doesn't fall into the same category at all. Not at all! We've been over that topic a thousand times. Remember our Grand Plan. We're working toward the perfection of mankind. We're working for Science, lad."

"So was Victor Frankenstein," Matthew muttered.

"Who? Frankenstein? Never heard of him."

"Never mind, sir." Matthew pulled away from the mirror and the doctor both. If he could survive the remainder of the night, he'd confront his fears squarely in the light of day.

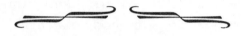

But the light of the coming day was muted, bearing only more rain. The doctor trotted off for the British Museum with promises of "concluding my current studies with dispatch." Still under the influence of his nightmare, Matthew abandoned his books to wander deeper and deeper into the ancient lanes of London. Head bowed, hat pulled low to ward off the weather, he tried to sort out the state of his soul. He made little progress. Perhaps it was due to the influence of the half-timbered buildings he passed. They seemed to lean toward him, closing in with their sightless windows and crumbling façades, bringing on further feelings of dread rather than relief. He never noticed the figure stealthily following him.

Time passed unheeded until Matthew pulled himself from his dark thoughts to discover he'd arrived in a warren of alleys dotted with low gin mills. Rough inhabitants scuttled around in clothes scarcely better than rags. Matthew stopped, raised the collar of his woolen topcoat against the chill, and took stock. He was lost. Undoubtedly lost. He turned to check the way he'd come.

"You!" he gasped.

The hulking form standing square in the path of his exit was as unspeakable as the surroundings. He was filthier than the last time Matthew had laid eyes on him. The jagged scar running down his face was a more vivid red. His teeth, when he opened his mouth in a grimace of a smile, were broken and black.

"What . . . what do you want?" the boy stammered.

A heavy hand clamped down on Matthew's shoulder. "For now, gin. Little master will join me, I trust?"

Matthew wriggled, then blindly punched out and even kicked, but the hold on him was like a vise. He was dragged into the nearest hellhole.

"I won't touch it!"

Trapped in the farthest, darkest corner of the
gin mill, Matthew hunched on a stool staring at
the grimy mug sitting before him on the warped
planks of the tabletop. It was filled to the brim
with a clear, pungent-smelling liquid.

"No need." The body snatcher stretched a
long arm to catch Matthew by the neck. With his
free hand he lifted the cup and jammed it to the
boy's mouth. Shoving the brim between his lips,
he forced the gin down his throat. Matthew
spluttered and gagged. Half the liquor drained
down his neck. But he swallowed the rest.

The body snatcher smiled evilly, downed his
own mug, and slammed it on to the boards.
"More!" he barked.

Matthew's head was reeling after the third
mug. His throat and stomach burned as if singed
by fire. He'd tried to spill as much as possible,
but the wasted gin angered his assailant. He'd had
several blows to the head to prove the fact. Hard
blows. His mind spun in circles around the same
theme: how to escape?

The body snatcher sat thigh to thigh next to
him, one hand now grasping Matthew's arm like

a manacle. It didn't keep the creature from downing his fourth gin with no noticeable effect. Why did each noggin of the liquor make the fiend appear even larger and more deadly? And Matthew smaller and more ensnared?

At last the body snatcher cleared his throat and spat on the dirty, straw-covered floor. "Now you will talk. You will tell me what I want to know."

"*Me* talk? What about you!"

His captor's fist shot up for another blow, then stopped midair. "Why not?" His evil grin was tinged with pride of accomplishment. "I did find you."

He waved permission for a question almost gallantly. And Matthew's hazy brain was swimming with questions. The first one burst forth. "How *did* you find us?"

A hollow growl of mirth. "The next packet leaving Philadelphia was fast. I set foot in Liverpool before you did in London. All this time since I've been tracking you." He reached for a fresh gin. "Not my usual line of work. But the pay is better."

Matthew shook his head in a valiant effort to clear it. The door was only a half dozen yards away, but the distance looked insurmountable.

He had to free his arm. He had to dodge around the table. Make that two tables. Or was it four? He seemed to be seeing double.

"Who is paying you?" he managed to choke out next, then added quickly, before his slurring tongue could get the best of him, "And for what?"

"Enough of your questions!" The villain slammed down his empty mug. "More!" he roared into the smokey haze of the room. "Hot grog this time. Against the chill."

A harried barmaid balanced steaming mugs on a tray, and carefully set out across the room, dodging clumps of weaving or slumped patrons along the way. None of them appeared to bother her in the least, not even the form of a young girl, skirts askew, passed out on the floor. But the woman did try to keep her distance from the body snatcher's fearful face. So engaged, she tripped on his long, outstretched legs. The tray in her grasp tipped and the hot liquor spilled, scalding him. He bellowed and raised a hand to slap the woman. It was the hand that had been imprisoning Matthew.

Matthew bolted—past the tables, out the door, and into the rain. Through his doubled vision he saw too many directions to run. He picked the closest doorway, the closest set of wooden stairs, and weaved toward them. Grasping twice for the railing before catching it, he clambered up the steps directly into a hallway reeking of filth. He promptly added to the smell by throwing up the contents of his stomach. He managed at least to back away a few feet before he toppled onto the floor. He lay there, wondering if dying was a better option than living. Then he blacked out.

Someone was washing his face. It was being done tenderly, systematically. From forehead to chin, then moving along to both cheeks. Matthew sighed and attempted to pry open an eye.

"Thank you, kind sir—"

The washing continued, this time over the eye in question. It opened.

"Thank you, again—" Matthew stopped. "A dog?" he whispered.

It was a dog, sort of. It must have belonged somewhere in the canine family, with possibly an added touch of bear. It was a great shaggy beast that hovered above him, more than half Matthew's size, but skinnier than even Matthew had been in the days before answering Dr. Cornwall's advertisement. The tongue came out again and Matthew gently brushed the muzzle aside. He tried to get up.

"Whoooh."

His head throbbed. His stomach wanted to retch. He was feverish. Every muscle in his body ached. He felt worse than he ever had in his life. What to do next? How to do it? The dog prodded his body under Matthew's arm. He accepted the assistance and tottered to his feet.

"Got to get home. Got to get back to Dr. Cornwall." He steadied himself as best he could, made a futile effort to grab for his pocket watch, then dropped his shaking fingers. "Don't know the time. Could that fiend still be waiting?"

The dog whimpered.

Matthew stroked its head. "Might as well come along, then. We can be lost together."

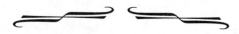

"Where in heaven's name have you been, Matthew? The British Museum closed hours ago. You know it's not safe on these streets at night. I've been frantic—"

Dr. Cornwall shut his mouth as Matthew staggered into their suite. He merely stared at the boy. Then he registered Matthew's companion. "And who might this creature be?"

Matthew sank into the nearest armchair. The dog sank on his haunches by his feet. "This is *Gin*. He just saved my life. Order something for him to eat, please? Nothing for me."

Cornwall's mouth gaped open and closed a few more times, then he reached for the bellpull.

"And order a bath, too, please. For both of us." Matthew sighed and closed his eyes.

Gin's growl at the knock on the door brought Matthew awake again. The doctor was already rushing to open it. A parade of hotel staff entered. The first waiter carried a folding table which he neatly opened and covered with a pristine white cloth. The second waiter laid a vast covered platter upon it. "Your steak tartare, gentlemen," he announced. "Ten orders of it, as you requested."

A third waiter set up another table which was soon covered with a soup tureen and teapot. Stewards followed with two tubs and steaming water. After Cornwall tipped them extravagantly, they all decamped.

The doctor stared at the boy still sprawled limply on the chair. "Food first, I should think." He gripped the huge covered platter, carefully eased it to the floor, and removed the lid with a flourish. He glanced at the alertly waiting dog. "Dinner is served, Gin."

Gin gave Matthew a look. The boy nodded. "Go ahead. It's all yours." The dog lunged at the meat.

Cornwall poured a cup of tea and handed it to Matthew. "I believe there's a story to be told, young man."

"Yes, sir, there is." Matthew sipped at the hot liquid. "For starters, he *can* talk—"

"Who can talk?"

"The body snatcher, of course."

Cornwall gasped and plopped into the facing chair. "Continue, lad. Pray continue."

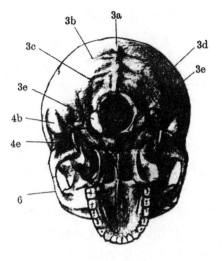

Inferior aspect

CHAPTER TWELVE

D R. CORNWALL AND MATTHEW BARRICADED THEM-
selves in their hotel suite for three days while
Matthew recovered. During that time they concentrated on feeding, grooming, and training
Gin—and plotting strategies. Matthew hadn't
forgotten the nightmare that had led him to his
adventure, but had come to the rational conclusion that never in a million years could he turn
into someone as vile as the body snatcher. For
one thing, his intolerance of strong spirits

wouldn't allow it. It also helped when Cornwall took the time to read the cause of Matthew's nightmare—Mary Shelley's *Frankenstein*. He snorted derisively as he completed the last page and snapped the novel shut.

"A pretty fantasy, lad. That's what this is." He tapped the covers of the book authoritatively. "And since when have I attempted to bring life back into my subjects? I wish to know what they were like for the benefit of future generations, true, but even I look upon death as final. My deceased friends have lived and worked through their own personal travails and now deserve whatever respite heaven—or hell—is willing to allow them."

The skulls of Henry Bedlow, Aaron Burr, and Nicholas Mordecai beamed down benignly from their posts atop the nearby mantelpiece. A great weight lifted from Matthew's chest.

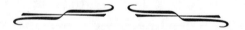

Before dawn on the fourth day, according to their carefully executed plan, Matthew and Dr. Cornwall slipped away from the hotel. They used a rear entrance, oversaw the loading of their precious war chest and other belongings into a waiting private coach, and set off from London for Dover and the English Channel.

Gin went with them. There was never any question of that. The great dog had left Matthew's side only twice a day since their first acquaintance—and that for necessary walks with their room steward. Now he wormed his way onto the coach seat next to Matthew, settled his hindquarters on the boy's lap, then balanced his front paws against the door to improve his view from the window. He took everything in stride, as if things were the way they were meant to be. Didn't dogs travel with their masters to the Continent on a regular basis?

Matthew patted the animal fondly. "He certainly has filled out in three days."

"And didn't you do the same when I put you on a diet of steak?" the doctor asked. "It's only fortunate we're currently in a position to feed him thus," he added dryly. "I'm not certain he'd stick around for oatmeal."

"I think Gin would stick around no matter what," Matthew replied. He hugged the beast and was rewarded with a wet kiss. "I never had a dog before." Something to love and be loved by. Matthew settled back into the cushions and gazed out a window himself. It didn't matter that it kept raining. Life was looking rosy.

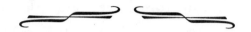

By midafternoon of the second day of their journey, the coach arrived in Canterbury. Cornwall gave instructions to the coachman to settle their belongings in a suitable inn, then dragged Matthew and Gin off on a tour of the medieval town.

"I've always wanted to visit Canterbury," Cornwall proclaimed. "Particularly the cathedral." He stopped before the massive edifice.

Matthew stretched his neck to take in the towers. "Why?" he asked. "It seems to be a very nice cathedral as cathedrals go, but—"

"*The Canterbury Tales*, lad. Chaucer's wonderful stories of medieval pilgrimage."

Matthew ruffled Gin's fur absently. "I'm afraid I don't know what—"

"Pilgrims were the tourists of the Middle Ages, my boy," the doctor automatically explained. "They abandoned everyday life and set out on the highways to visit holy sites of saints. Most were genuinely religious, but some just had wanderlust. It was the only way you could safely travel in those days, always in large enough groups to fend off roving bandits." He waved at the huge wooden door of the cathedral before them. "And here was the most famous

English place of pilgrimage, lodging the greatest of English saints, Thomas à Becket. Come along." He grabbed Matthew's arm, then, with a glance at the dog, halted at the entrance. "I don't believe it would be appropriate for Gin to enter these sacred walls."

"Why not? Didn't God make the animals, too?"

"He certainly did, but the clergy and faithful might still look askance."

Unwillingly, Matthew turned to Gin. He pointed to the steps outside the door. "Sit, Gin. Stay. We won't be long."

Gin whined, but settled himself as directed.

Inside the cathedral the nave opened in lovely Gothic arches. Cornwall spent little time admiring them, however. Instead, he shoved Matthew along the ambulatory till he stopped before a large marble sarcophagus elevated from the floor.

"Here it is," he sighed.

Matthew said nothing. The sight of the sarcophagus was enough. It set off warning bells in his head. Anytime Dr. Cornwall got excited about a tomb, he began worrying about the obvious implications. Already Matthew was measuring the size in his head, considering the weight of the slab of marble that topped it, wondering where they could find a block and tackle to raise it, and, most important, what time of night the deed could safely be done.

But Cornwall was deep in other thoughts. "Here is where the blood of the Archbishop of Canterbury, St. Thomas à Becket himself, was spilled. Back in 1170 it was. Becket was feuding with his old friend King Henry the Second, and Henry's henchmen performed the evil deed for him while Becket was saying Mass." Cornwall patted the marble fondly. "Instant martyrdom, instant sainthood."

Then he spoke the words Matthew had been anticipating and dreading.

"What I wouldn't give for his skull!"

"But a saint!" Matthew protested. "You can't disturb a saint!"

"Wherein lies holiness, lad? Has anyone ever measured and analyzed the faculties? How much better might it be for humankind if my mission were saints rather than charismatic thinkers and leaders of a more worldly bent." Cornwall shook his head sadly. "Alas, my training takes me along a different path. And as Becket himself proves, it was never meant to be."

Matthew's pent-up breath heaved out. "You mean—"

"I mean his bones no longer reside here, never mind his skull. What wasn't snatched by pilgrims and pulverized into relics was thoroughly destroyed during Henry the Eighth's Reformation."

"Ah." Matthew touched the cool marble reverently. Now he could imagine the drama of the fight to the death. Imagine pilgrims, weary from their travels, crawling on hands and knees to venerate this place. The arches above him opened wider. Sunlight streamed through the high windows. The rays reached the empty tomb itself. "St. Thomas à Becket. I'll remember him."

"You do that, lad. Remember the layout, too. For future reference."

With a groan, Matthew began calculating all over again. Cornwall's message was clear. If not this sarcophagus, then another one lay in their future. Thank goodness it would never be that of a saint.

In the morning they arrived at the sea and embarked on a ship for France. The crossing was turbulent, but Matthew and Gin stood staunchly in the stern, wind-whipped and excited, watching the chalk-white cliffs of Dover recede as the distance between them and their nemesis widened. Crossing a good stretch of water always seemed hopeful to Matthew. Safe.

As for Dr. Cornwall, he retreated to a cabin where he could turn green in peace. When he stumbled off the ship and into France, the doctor seemed close to kissing that solid French earth. Instead, he made one of his sudden declarations.

"Paris can wait. It's my turn to recover, and we'll do it in Calais."

Matthew stared back across the English Channel. Suddenly the thirty-five mile distance seemed much shorter, much less secure. "But what of the body snatcher, sir? Surely by now he's discovered that we're gone. Surely his first search would be toward France—"

Cornwall looked definitively bilious. "And why not toward Oxford or Cambridge?"

"Sir, I said he could talk, but I never said how well he could *think*. I'm quite certain his head doesn't include knowledge of higher education, of places like Oxford or Cambridge."

Cornwall swayed and Matthew stretched his arms to steady him.

"Remind me to get my hands on that head sometime," the doctor muttered. "It could prove quite interesting, a link to the past rather than the future of mankind. There's a certain simian qual- ity—" He wiped a sheen of sweat from his brow. "Now, be a good lad and go practice your French. Deal with the luggage and an inn." He sank onto the nearest bollard, moaning, "Never have kip- pers for breakfast just before a sea voyage!"

Matthew finally budged the doctor from the coast of France and inland toward Paris. Winter was settling with gray persistence over the barren fields they crossed. It seemed as if all the farmers and their families were securely tucked inside the wall-enclosed houses that dotted the countryside like small fortresses. Matthew's cheerfulness evaporated. Visions assailed him—visions of fam- ilies snugly gathered around their warm fires, like his own once had been. It was nearing the first anniversary of his great loss, and Matthew felt himself in mourning with the season. So much had happened in the brief year since—so much more after he'd met Dr. Cornwall. Huddled within his topcoat as the drafty coach lumbered on, he reflected on it all.

As if to intensify his melancholy thoughts, some instinct kept nudging him to turn to the rear, to watch his back. To watch his master's back, too. There was no one else to protect Asa B. Cornwall, and the man was far too trusting. The boy sighed. The doctor was all the family he now had.

"Hey!"

Matthew was drawn from his thoughts by a sudden loving lick from Gin.

"I was wrong, wasn't I?" he whispered in the dog's ear. "I've got you now, too."

He wrestled playfully with the huge animal. "And you'll defend me, defend the doctor, too, won't you? Against all the wicked body snatchers in the world!"

Gin yipped a cheerful agreement, waking Cornwall from his doze in the seat opposite them.

"Eh? What's that you said, Matthew?"

"Nothing, sir. Just explaining Gin's duties to him."

"Fine, fine." The doctor's eyes slid shut once more.

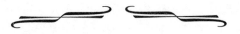

As Paris appeared before them, Dr. Cornwall came out of the sleepy coma that seemed to have overtaken him. The satchel containing the precious manuscript was pulled to his side again. Luster returned to his eyes.

"This is it, my boy. The city that will make or break my theories. Make or break Part Two!"

Matthew shoved Gin's bulk from his lap and began brushing dog hairs from his trousers. "Not the city, sir, the person." He bit the bullet. "Who is it to be?"

Cornwall smirked. "You mean you haven't guessed?"

"I've had other things on my mind, sir."

"Think, lad! Think back to our first acquaintance. Who among the French do I venerate above all?"

"Napoleon?" Matthew tried.

"Close, but not correct. Guess again."

Matthew shook his head. He wasn't feeling that playful.

Cornwall's face fell. "I was hoping for a little more enthusiasm, boy. Why have we been studying the language, after all?"

"To deal with clients?"

"Pooh. Icing on the cake. Emperor Charles the Fifth used to say that in proportion to the number of languages a man knew, he was so many more times a man. One truly learns a language to get beyond the obvious, to get into the very souls of a people. The French most of all. Their language shows their thinking, their philosophy—"

"Voltaire!" Matthew burst out. "You're going for Voltaire!"

"Bravo, lad. Bravo." The doctor's eyes were twinkling again. "Anyone can have his bust, but I shall have Voltaire's skull!"

"Are you sure he's buried in Paris, sir?"

"Of course! I've done my research."

"Where?" The coach was beginning to slow.

Cornwall hugged the secret to his body as he hugged his manuscript. "In good time, lad, in good time."

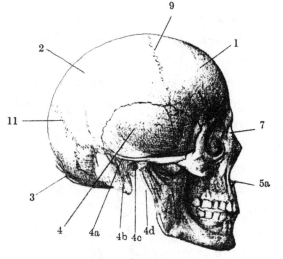

Lateral aspect

CHAPTER THIRTEEN

"I‍T REALLY IS A PITY YOU DIDN'T HOLD OFF YOUR escape from our body snatcher just a tad longer," the doctor complained. "At least till you'd learned the name of *his* employer. Or the reason behind all the nonsense—"

It was the first time Asa B. Cornwall had stated the obvious. It wasn't the first time Matthew had agonized over it. He'd worked the abduction over and over in his mind until it began to look like a very bad play. A melodrama. He never could imagine any other ending, any other way out than the one he'd taken. And the doctor had been most sympathetic about the entire episode. He was really only remarking on it now because of the more stringent security measures Matthew was attempting to foist on him.

"—And we wouldn't have had the inconvenience," Cornwall continued. "This is the third hotel you've dragged me to!" The doctor finally spit out his true grievance as he motioned around the suite they were examining. "The first one didn't have any corner suites—"

Matthew nodded agreement. "We've got to have a bird's-eye view from at least two directions. If the body snatcher is lurking on the street, we want to be able to spot him before we go out."

Cornwall resumed his list of gripes. "The second hotel's concierge didn't meet with your approval—"

"Didn't you inspect the man? He had the very look of a villain! He would have sold us for a fistful of pennies."

"*Centimes*," the doctor corrected. "The French equivalent. But I disagree with you. I think he might have held out for a fistful of *francs*." Cornwall cracked a smile. "So what's wrong with this place? Their vault looks like the Bank of England's. Their staff seems the very soul of discretion." He pointed at the corner sitting room the two stood in. "Windows with a view." The doctor walked over to the closest one. "A very pleasant view, I might add. The Seine River, Notre Dame Cathedral." He wandered to the perpendicular window. "And if one stretches a little, one can almost make out the Pantheon only a half dozen blocks to the south. The Latin Quarter does seem an excellently central location." He turned away to notice that Gin had already staked out a satin-covered settee. "Your dog likes it, too, and"—he paused for the proper emphasis—"the hotel's chef is rumored to be superb." Cornwall glared at Matthew. "I repeat, what's wrong with this one?"

Matthew laughed. "Nothing, sir. Nothing at all." He turned to the porter waiting patiently behind them. "*C'est bien,*" he said. "*Nos bagages, s'il vous plaît.*"

Cornwall insisted on a proper tour of the city before getting down to business. They spent a week with a hired carriage at their beck and call, viewing the art, the boulevards, Napoleon's Arc de Triomphe, the Obelisk in the Place de la Concorde. Cornwall was particularly intrigued by this square and kept wandering around its edges.

"Why?" Matthew finally asked.

"Heads, as usual," the doctor grinned. "Can you picture being here during the Revolution?" He waved with animation. "Over there, that's where the guillotine was erected for the execution of Louis the Sixteenth!"

He spun to point across the open space. "And there. There, a few months later, it was set up again. This time the heads of Marie Antoinette, Madame du Barry, Danton, Robespierre, and a large number of their friends—they all rolled." He shook his own head in wonder. "The French called their device 'the nation's razor.' Only imagine, lad, all those heads . . ."

Nausea overcame Matthew. The instant image in his mind of mild, kindly Dr. Asa B. Cornwall plucking freshly severed heads from the basket below the guillotine was enough to make him want to chuck his very civilized French breakfast. Thank goodness he hadn't been here. Thank goodness he hadn't yet been born. Acquiring nice, dried-out skulls of decently deceased people suddenly seemed a far less unpleasant task—

possibly even a commendable one, as it did have the betterment of mankind as its aim. He wasn't sorry to leave the Place de la Concorde.

As Cornwall continued to give their driver instructions, Matthew noticed that their sweeps around the city were becoming smaller and smaller, the circle closing in on the Ile de la Cité, then the Left Bank, and finally the neighborhood bordering it—their own Latin Quarter—which seemed to surround the Pantheon. Matthew began to strongly suspect where the philosopher Voltaire was buried.

They made their first visit to the Pantheon on Christmas Eve.

"Call it indulgence, lad, but I've been saving this up. After all these years, it's my present, my Christmas present."

Matthew sighed as he gave Gin his usual instructions to *stay* and he and the doctor entered the vast neoclassic building. "So he is here. Voltaire."

"Indeed." Cornwall swept toward an enormous dome rising above the center of the floor. "All this was built as a church but was turned into a *pantheon*, a home of the gods, during the

French Revolution. Where else could Voltaire be buried?"

Matthew took in the columns and friezes lining the walls. "Is he tucked behind one of these pillars?"

"No, no." The doctor was still rushing forward. "In the crypt, of course. In the basement."

And then they were in the dim recesses of the crypt itself, wandering in hushed reverence past rows of massive sarcophagi. Cornwall squinted at the gold lettering of each in turn, was briefly distracted by the remains of Rousseau, then finally stopped cold before the small alcove that held a dark marble tomb. He clutched at his heart.

Matthew allowed the doctor his moment of respect, then grew alarmed by his silence and the sudden tremble of his master's body. "Are you all right, sir?"

Cornwall stirred enough to rub at his eyes. "Emotion, lad. Just overcome by emotion. To have arrived at last at the final resting place of one of the greatest intellects in recorded history—" He tottered and Matthew jumped to prop him up. "It's just *overwhelming*."

"As you say, sir." Matthew was overwhelmed, too. He'd taken his first good look at the tomb. The marble lid of the sarcophagus must weigh at least a ton. Maybe two. The huge ball of marble sculpted in the center of the slab probably weighed five hundred pounds all on its own. This job was going to be impossible.

Cornwall noted none of his assistant's concern. He stood frozen in rapt devotion until an ancient guard came shuffling through the crypt. "*Fermé*," the old man croaked. "*Fermé pour la fête*."

Matthew gently shook the doctor's arm. "Sir? I think they're closing early for Christmas, sir."

The doctor pulled himself away with effort. "Yes, yes, of course. We'd best return for our own celebrations, Matthew."

It was a quiet Christmas for Matthew. He and the doctor exchanged a few gifts around the fire in their sitting room. Matthew had managed to find a small phrenology bust for his master to replace those they'd left behind in New York. It pleased them both because all the faculties were spelled out in French. Gin received a fine leather collar and leash for which he was perhaps not as grateful, but the French did seem to prefer their pets under control. Dr. Cornwall presented Matthew with copies of Voltaire's *Candide*.

"In English and French both, my boy. So you can start in on one while your reading skills improve in the other."

Their festivities completed, Cornwall donned his favorite old frayed velvet jacket, settled in a comfortable chair, propped his slippered feet before the fire, and began to dream aloud.

"New Year's Eve, Matthew. I should like to collect Voltaire on New Year's Eve. It would be an excellent omen for the New Year, beginning the new Decade of Science—1840!"

"But—" Matthew lay sprawled on the rug next to Gin. "That's less than a week away!"

"More than enough time to work out our plan of operations," the doctor glibly replied. "More than enough time to acquire the necessary equipment. I expect no great difficulties."

"*He* expects no great difficulties," Matthew complained in Gin's ear. "*He* hasn't got to work out the engineering. This isn't a simple matter of pick and shovel!"

"I can't hear you, lad. Speak up."

"I was talking to Gin, sir."

"Oh. Well, as I was saying, I expect no great difficulties. Everything has been with us thus far. The weather has been extraordinarily pleasant for December. Crisp but fair. Who could have dreamed of sunshine in Paris after all that rain en route? We've seen neither hide nor hair of the body snatcher, either—"

That caused Matthew to stir and sit. "I wish you wouldn't speak of him so lightly, sir. Or speak of him at all."

"Why not? What's this sudden reticence?"

Matthew shook his head. "I don't know. It just came over me. A feeling that it might be like tempting—"

"Fate, lad?" Cornwall chuckled comfortably from his chair. "Nonsense. I feel we've been quite clever this time. Once burned, twice shy."

"It's been more than once," Matthew muttered.

"Eh, what's that?"

"Merry Christmas, sir."

"Why, yes. Merry Christmas to you, too, lad."

It began to snow during Christmas night. Matthew tossed restlessly in his bed, then got up to peek from his window. He'd sensed what was happening from the stillness that had settled over the city. And there it was: snow falling gently over the silhouette of Notre Dame in the distance; snow gliding down onto the waters of the Seine.

Snowflakes were whitening the rooftops in between the river and their hotel; settling on the figure hunched into a doorway across the very street from their building. Matthew's eyes zeroed in on the figure, but it wasn't necessary. He already knew who it was.

The wind rose out of nowhere to send the snow into eddies. More snow, heavier snow, followed on the wind's tail. Matthew shivered and crawled back under his covers. At least he was warm. Perhaps by morning the body snatcher would be frozen into his doorway, like one of the statues that littered Paris everywhere one looked. Burrowing deeper within his cocoon, Matthew drifted into sleep.

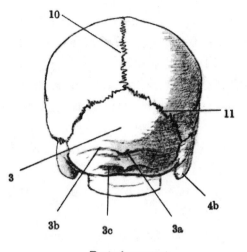

Posterior aspect

CHAPTER FOURTEEN

"HE'S GONE!"

Matthew pulled his head from the window to confront Cornwall, who was draped over the sitting room's little breakfast table, blissfully dunking a fresh roll into his morning *café au lait*.

"Eh? Who's gone?"

Matthew shrugged. Perhaps it was all fated. The entire absurd course of his life. Perhaps he was never even meant to reach the exalted age of thirteen in a few weeks' time. He breathed the name in defeat. "The body snatcher."

The doctor picked up his coffee bowl and slowly drained it. "Been having nightmares again, lad?"

"Maybe." Matthew shrugged again. "But it didn't feel like a nightmare. He was right across the street from my bedroom window last night—right across from our hotel's entrance. I'd swear to it."

Cornwall's raised eyebrows put a little fire back into Matthew.

"I know the difference between dreams and true life! I'll bet his footprints are still there. I'll prove it!" He ran for his coat and began struggling into it.

"Slow down, lad. How much snow has fallen since you purportedly saw our illustrious fiend?"

Matthew unwillingly returned to the window. "A great deal."

"And it's still snowing, correct?"

"Furiously," he grudgingly allowed.

Cornwall pulled out the adjoining chair. "Sit. Eat your breakfast. We can't afford the body snatcher at this point. The footprints—if there were any—will be long gone. Erased. Do the same with your fears. Banish them. We seem to have encountered a genuine blizzard. Never even knew the French had them. This obviously calls for a quiet day of repose and contemplation."

Matthew slung off his coat, stomped over to the table, and threw himself into the chair.

"Tsk, tsk. Developing a temper, lad? I'm not certain this delicate French furniture can bear the brunt."

Matthew growled, causing Gin to raise his head questioningly and trot over from his spot by the fire. "All right then, sir." He ran his fingers through the dog's fur to calm himself. Cornwall wanted to ignore the incident. Cornwall hadn't been the one mauled by the body snatcher in London. "What exactly are we supposed to be reposing and contemplating over?"

"Why, the device that will raise Voltaire to glory, of course." Cornwall shoved the breakfast things to the edge of the table. "Why don't you fetch my pen and inkwell? Some paper, too."

Matthew fetched, then rejoined the doctor with slightly better grace. Let Cornwall get his silly head of Voltaire, and maybe they could return to the road again. Put some more distance between themselves and their pursuer. Certainly the two of them should be able to outthink that brute. Maybe they had to make their own fate. Meanwhile, there was the doctor's latest project to deal with. Matthew tried to rub the knots of tension from his neck. Best get down to business.

"The way I see it, sir, that ridiculous ball atop Voltaire's lid might be a godsend. If we were to acquire a tripod, and some tackle and pulleys and such, we could attach it all to the ball, then pry the slab loose. We don't have to actually raise the whole thing, either. Just set it ajar enough to have a peek inside."

His father had firmly believed that a master workman always needed a picture of the job he was commencing. Matthew reached for the paper and pen.

"Let me sketch it out for you."

Many hours later, the two were still bent over the table. By this time a dozen sketches were strewn around. Matthew finally sat back.

"There it is, then. Perhaps it is possible. It leaves us with only four major problems."

"Yes?" Cornwall asked.

Matthew ticked them off on his fingers. "First, acquiring the equipment. Second, secreting it inside the crypt without being caught. Third, hiding ourselves within the building until it's closed for the night." He stopped.

"And the fourth?"

"That should be obvious, sir." Matthew stared out the closest window at the snow still falling. "Evading the body snatcher until we've accomplished it all."

Cornwall digested Matthew's words, then cleared his throat with a great *hurumph*. The boy stared at him, waiting.

"It occurs to me, lad—"

"Yes?"

"It occurs to me that your whole heart isn't going to be in our latest project until we've dealt with number four. So maybe we ought to take care of that first." The doctor stroked his bald head thoughtfully. "Perhaps we've been going about this body snatcher business from entirely the wrong perspective."

"How's that?"

"Well, he's currently got us on the defensive. He's always had us on the defensive. It begins to grate."

Matthew tipped back in his frail chair. "So?"

"So, perhaps it's time for us to take the offensive. Turn the tables. Dog *him*."

"*Dog* him. Dog the body snatcher!" Matthew's eyes fell on Gin, and his entire face lit up. "Yes! Of course!" He threw up his hands, kicked his feet—and promptly crashed onto the floor with the chair in splinters around him.

Cornwall glanced down. "I warned you the furniture was weak. A little less enthusiasm until we've come up with a *modus operandi*, please."

Matthew was posted by the window, only his eyes peeking between the slit of the heavy drapery. The snow had stopped at last and night was rapidly approaching. He'd been watching weary Parisiens trudge home through the muck for well over an hour. He studied each person's height, clothing, and entire prospect until they disappeared from view. Mostly sweepers and anonymous workingmen had been out. He watched more closely as another figure came into view: tall, broad, with his head covered by a wide-brimmed hat. There was something indefinably brutish about this one. He willed the man to come closer, to pause with a quick glance toward their third floor windows. The hat slipped back for a moment.

"Got you!" Matthew exulted. He waited for the man to duck into a doorway. Waited as he pulled a bottle from beneath his cloak and tipped it to his lips for a long swig.

"Dr. Cornwall!"

"What's that?" Asa B. Cornwall's head jerked up from his chest. He'd been nodding in his chair by the fire.

"He's here, sir! May we go out now? May we?"

The doctor hauled himself up. "Let me have a look first." He approached the window and cautiously parted the drapery. "Yes, it does seem to be our quarry." His eyes wandered farther along the street. "Not the only character skulking about in the cold, either."

"What do you mean?" Matthew shoved the drapes wider.

"Over there, on the far corner—" Cornwall squinted, then stepped back, suddenly pale.

"It's only some foreign-looking man," Matthew said. "Maybe from India? That turban—"

"Yes, the turban!" the doctor exclaimed. "Oh dear, I wish we had a spyglass. Can you make out the emblem on the center of the turban?"

Matthew nodded. "It almost looks as if it's some kind of a flower."

"A rose," Cornwall stated. "It has to be. The *Rosicrucians*! Certain of their adepts wear such a turban, such a sign. I *knew* their leader, their Imperator, resided in Normandy, but I assumed the society was going through one of its sleeper periods, even when I rashly suggested the group as possible conspirators so long ago back in New York—"

"What are you going on about, Doctor?" Matthew glanced through the window again. "Your turbaned conspirator just hailed a carriage and is gone. I wish I could say the same for the body snatcher. May we go after him now? *Please.*"

Asa B. Cornwall shook his head as if trying to remove its woolliness. "Conspiracy theories do seem to feed on themselves. I suppose we ought to concentrate on one at a time." He took a deep breath. "By all means. Let's get it over with so I can keep my New Year's Eve rendezvous."

Gin was already standing expectantly by the door. Matthew grabbed his coat, opened the door, then leaned down to give the dog a hug. "It's hunting time, Gin. I hope you like your beast rare!"

Gin yipped and lunged for the stairs.

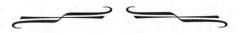

"It would have been easier if we'd just lingered unobtrusively in the lobby until the scoundrel made a move," Cornwall complained as he huffed through several feet of drifted snow behind Matthew. "But no, you had to leave the hotel by the rear servants' entrance. You had to walk the entire circumference of the block. And now we're going to freeze while we do our surveillance—"

"Save your breath, sir. Gin needed the exercise anyhow, and we're almost there." Matthew completed the distance to the corner, then held Gin back with one hand while he poked his head around the building.

"Hah! The fiend's still waiting, turned slightly away from us." He stared, then continued his report. "He's pulling out that bottle of his. It must be more gin—"

The dog perked his ears expectantly.

"Brandy." Cornwall panted up behind Matthew and leaned heavily on the walking stick he'd decided to bring. "It's more traditional for the French. I could do with a tot of it myself. It's devilishly cold out here!"

"Hush," Matthew hissed. "He's tossing the bottle into the street. It must be empty."

The doctor poked his own head around the corner as if to verify Matthew's report. Or maybe it was only to search for mysterious turbans. He pulled back again. "Now, remember what you promised me, lad. We're going to stand watch until he decides to move. Then we're going to follow him until we find his place of abode. All very discreetly. Once that has been accomplished, we can slip from the hotel by daylight— under his very nose while *he* thinks he's keeping watch on us—and begin to make inquiries into his habits and acquaintances." Cornwall shifted his weight in the snow. "We might even inspect his room—in his absence and again most discreetly. There must be some correspondence with his employer. Our object is to learn his motivation, and that is absolutely all. That knowledge will give us power. Never do we wish to confront the villain head on—"

"He's reaching under his cloak again." With the body snatcher within grasp at last, Matthew stopped listening to the doctor. "Aha! Another bottle. He's pulling the cork with his teeth—"

Something suddenly rose in Matthew's chest. The sight of his mortal enemy blatantly standing there guzzling spirits was more than he could take. The man was undoubtedly working out vile plans in his viler mind. Burglary, kidnapping. He'd already done all those. What was he plotting next?

As the nightmare came back to him, as the memory of the blows suffered in the London gin mill made his head ache once more, emotions buried inside Matthew exploded. The body snatcher was implacable. He'd never quit. His sheer relentlessness became overwhelming.

Matthew let out a war whoop and charged around the corner and into the street. Gin raced beside him. Cornwall hobbled to their rear, brandishing his stick and yelling, "Stop! Stop!"

The body snatcher pivoted toward the racket. Catching the unexpected sight, he spat the cork from his teeth and grabbed the bottle defensively by its neck. His free hand slipped beneath his cloak yet again. When it reappeared, it was holding a long, slender object which flashed in the light of a streetlamp. A knife!

Matthew barreled on. He was twenty yards away, ten, five. The body snatcher strode out to meet him, arms stretched, weapons poised. The man, the cape, his shadow in the lamplight—they suddenly filled the empty street.

"Matthew, in the name of heaven, stop!"

Cornwall's voice registered, but did not stop Matthew. He was totally focused. Focused on the low, jutting brow, the jagged scar, the graveyard scent emanating toward him. He had no weapon but his head, so he rammed like a bull, butting directly into the body snatcher's stomach.

There was a *woof* of surprise. Then Matthew dimly perceived the solid glass of the brandy bottle closing in on one side, the shining knife on the other. He concentrated on the unearthly sounds coming from Gin's throat. Through the baying came a sharp crack. But the crack didn't seem connected to him in any way, because Matthew was already floating through a long, dark tunnel.

"Discretion, lad, discretion."

When Matthew's eyes opened, Asa B. Cornwall was hovering over him. The word was repeated again, most sorrowfully. Matthew blinked.

"Where am I?" he murmured.

"In your bed, of course. In our suite, in the hotel. In Paris, France."

"I'm not sure I needed to know all of that." Matthew shook his head, then winced. He reached up to finger a wide swath of bandage wrapped around his skull. "How did this . . . ?"

Cornwall sighed. "The concierge fetched a doctor for you, after the *gendarmes* were all gone."

"*Gendarmes?* Police? Why . . . ?"

The doctor sighed again. "The police came on

the run when they heard Gin's unearthly ruckus.
The timing was fortuitous, at least. They found
the body snatcher attacking *you*, rather than *you*
most immoderately attacking the body snatcher.
Didn't I tell you, boy? Didn't I beg you?
Discretion, I said. Discretion, above all—"

It began to come back to Matthew, in brief
flashes. The cold, the snow, his bitter enemy. The
unquenchable urge . . . He reached his fingers up
to touch the bandage again. Winced again.

"Go ahead, suffer," Cornwall chided. "You
brought it on yourself. A concussion, the doctor
diagnosed. Bed rest for a week." He patted at the
limp strands of hair across his pate in frustration. "I know I analyzed you as having a streak of
Combativeness at our first meeting, but never
have I so misjudged the strength of the organ."
He touched a spot above Matthew's ear. Matthew
yelped.

"There," Cornwall continued. "That's where
our body snatcher soundly conked you with his
brandy bottle. Smack on your organ of
Destructiveness. That, at least, should be a bless-
ing. If the faculty wasn't recessive before, it certainly should be now. Maybe he smashed a little
more sense into your head."

Matthew groaned. "Where's Gin?"

The doctor gave a little whistle and the dog trotted up, a huge gristly bone clutched between his jaws. His eyes lit at the sight of his master awake at last. He gently placed the bone on the bed as an offering.

"Thank you, Gin," Matthew managed. He moved his eyes back to the doctor. Cornwall read the question in them.

"Yes, the bone was a reward. The animal performed nobly, to say the least. By the time I arrived with my walking stick raised, he nearly had the villain's knife arm for supper. Unfortunately, not before—"

"Not before what?" Matthew asked.

The doctor sighed for a third time. "Best to get it over with, and there's no time like the present, I suppose." He trotted off and eventually returned with his shaving mirror. "Here."

"What?"

"Have a look."

Matthew stared into the mirror. As his eyes slowly focused, he took in the bandage slanted across his head, black curls edging the bright whiteness. He could live with that. It gave him a rather rakish, piratical look. Besides, it wouldn't be forever. He lowered the mirror. Bloodshot eyes, nose still intact—

"*What!*"

Cornwall rocked back on his heels, silent for once.

"But, but—"

The body snatcher had given him a scar. It wasn't nearly as long, or nearly as jagged as the villain's, but there it was. A scar, neatly stitched. From the corner of his eye, swooping several inches down the length of his cheekbone.

Cornwall found his voice. "Chapine, the doctor, said you were quite fortunate not to lose the eye. He also said he'd caught the cut in time. That he was thought to have the best sewing hand in all of his profession. 'My work is like the finest embroidery,' he said." Cornwall rushed on. "He said it would heal like a dueling scar. You would be admired by all the young ladies—"

"*My dream!*" Matthew whispered in stunned horror. "*I'm marked like the body snatcher!*"

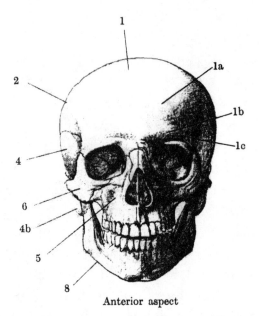

Anterior aspect

CHAPTER FIFTEEN

"ON THE BRIGHT SIDE, LAD, ON THE BRIGHT SIDE—"

Morning came, and Matthew woke from the sleep that had followed his great shock. As he lay propped against his pillows, a weak ray of sunshine caressed the stitches of his scar.

"What bright side?" he groaned.

Cornwall chuckled. "You never asked me about the body snatcher."

"What about him?"

"You never inquired after his disposition.

Come, come, boy, surely your wounds haven't left you that dull!"

Matthew stirred faintly. "All right, what happened to him?"

Asa B. Cornwall did a little jig. "I've just had word from the concierge. The scoundrel is safely tucked away in the depths of a foul French dungeon. At some point he'll go on trial for attempted robbery and bodily damage. And you know the French justice system—"

"I don't," Matthew disagreed.

"Guilty until proven innocent, lad. And who could be guiltier than he? Of everything. With any luck he'll be stashed away for life." The doctor chortled. "We're free, Matthew Morrissey. Free to proceed with the next phase of our operations. Free to proceed with Part Two of my *magnum opus!*"

"What about your secret society of conspirators?"

"The Rosicrucians? Pooh. Just my imagination acting up. Paris is an international city. There's bound to be a few turbans walking about. Think of it, lad. No more looking over our shoulders. We're truly free at last!"

Matthew scratched at his scar. "It itches. It will probably always itch."

Cornwall frowned. "Lie there and feel sorry for yourself, if that's what you want. Sink into your slough of despond. I'm off for a few hours to acquire some equipment. The New Year is fast closing in on us."

After two more days of recovery, Matthew could no longer justify his extended sulk. It was boring, lying in bed. Besides, the equipment growing in piles around the suite began to pique his curiosity. He rolled from his pillows and began prowling through it.

"There's stuff here we didn't talk about."

Cornwall stretched up from a pile. "Back in the land of the living, are we?"

Matthew ignored the jibe. "These." He poked at what looked like cases for musical instruments. "What are they?"

"French horn cases, of course. A perfect fit for pulleys and tackle."

"And what about these capes? We've never worn capes."

"They're coming back in style, lad. Haven't you noticed? And they can hide a multitude of sins—or equipment, as the case may be. A little lesson I learned from your body snatcher."

"He's not *my* body snatcher!"

"Oh, piffle. It's time you got over your snit.

The poultices Chapine sent up have worked wonders on your souvenir. The inflammation has disappeared and the stitches are healing nicely. You'll be left with a virile, yet discreet slash—and an excellent story to tell your children someday."

Matthew walked to a mirror. It was true. The scar was healing. His head felt better, too. He slowly unraveled the bandage. "When do we start ferrying equipment?"

Cornwall smiled. "I thought we might make our first visit this afternoon. I'm tired of walking your great beast by myself, and some air might do you the world of good."

By New Year's Eve all the supplies had been transported and carefully secreted behind unremarkable sarcophagi in the crypt of the Pantheon. Cornwall had the hotel's chef pack them a celebratory basket filled with all sorts of goodies suitable for a New Year's feast. He handed the basket to Matthew.

"You take this, lad. I'll carry my usual satchel."

"I'm supposed to carry this picnic into the Pantheon in full daylight?"

"Why not? It's the most innocent thing in the world. Hurry along now, in case they decide to close early again."

Gin beat them to the door as usual. Matthew gave a cry as he looked at the dog. "What about him? We can't leave him outside on the Pantheon's steps for the entire night!"

Cornwall pushed the dog's muzzle from the crack in the door. "As much as I'd like Gin to share in our victory this evening, he's the one object impossible to hide. But not to worry, I've already paid the porter to take him for a walk and feed him while we're attending a private party. And what a party it will be, Matthew Morrissey. What a party!"

"*Fermé . . . Fermé!*"

The usual ancient guard doddered through the Pantheon's crypt. From his post behind Voltaire's tomb, Matthew noticed his moldering soldier's uniform for the first time. It was complete with several faded ribbons, probably from the Napoleonic Wars. The old man was out of sight now. His labored steps echoed on the stairs leading from the crypt. The iron door at the top clanged shut with a finality that sent a shiver of dread through Matthew. It was nearly impossible working out the French system of holidays. What if the Pantheon were to be closed for New Year's

Day? What if they were stuck in here with nothing but venerable dead bodies for forty-eight hours or more?

Cornwall stirred next to him. "Can you remember where we hid the lamp, Matthew? The light from these half windows is fading fast."

"Behind that mathematician, I think."

"Condorcet?"

"Let me look."

It was those very arched half windows in the alcove behind Voltaire that Matthew had to deal with first. Balancing on tiptoe atop the sarcophagus, he brushed glue from a little pot onto the edges of the stone wall, then carefully spread thick sheets of paper till no telltale light could escape to the outside. The doctor was prowling behind him.

"You left a gap over to the right, lad."

"That's almost impossible to reach!"

"We must be perfectionists, mustn't we? No sense in giving away the game at this point."

Matthew stretched farther.

When Cornwall was completely satisfied, they set up the tripod. The doctor had found a carpenter willing to follow one of Matthew's diagrams, cutting the lengths of wood into pieces, then scoring the separate ends like screws. It was only a matter of minutes to fit and twist the segments back together. Next Matthew set up the rigging. Finally he stood back to admire the lot.

"There. I think it's ready." He smiled in spite of himself. The portable tripod he'd invented—in fact, the entire results of his plan—looked quite professional. Now if only Voltaire's decorative marble ball would withstand the strain of the tons of stone to which it was attached . . .

Cornwall consulted his pocket watch. "Tiptop work, lad. It's not even eleven yet. I propose we partake of our celebratory feast now, then do the deed as the golden hour approaches."

"Fine with me, sir. I could eat a horse."

The doctor pulled the food basket closer to the lamp. He untucked the tablecloth covering it and spread it neatly upon the cold marble floor, humming as he worked. Pots were set upon the cloth. Cornwall stuck his nose in one after the other.

"What have we here? And here?" He grinned at Matthew. "You'll have to settle for several patés, a lovely Brie—" He unwrapped a cloth from another hunk of cheese. "And some very potent Roquefort. Not to mention—" He was burrowing into the basket's depths. "Hah! Cold chicken. Sliced ham." He slapped down a long loaf. "Bread. And the crowning touch." Cornwall chuckled as he produced a bottle.

"Not *gin*, sir!"

"Never. Champagne. And two glasses." He flourished them. "Everything we need, lad. But before we dig in—"

Cornwall fussed with the bottle until the wired cork burst like a shot to the ceiling. Bubbles flowed down the doctor's arm. He splashed the liquid into the glasses. "A toast. We must have a toast!"

Matthew eyed his glass with suspicion. "If you say so, sir."

"Don't turn prudish, lad. You needn't drink more than a sip." He raised his glass. "To Voltaire!"

"To Voltaire!" Matthew repeated. Then he attacked the food.

"I'm going to try the pulley now. Are you ready, sir? All you've got to do is shove the lid a little to one side once it's loosened."

Cornwall was squinting at his watch again. "Eleven-fifty. Perfect timing. The hour is almost upon us." He snapped the timepiece shut and tucked it back into his pocket. Then he stood staring at the tomb.

"What's the matter, sir?"

"Nerves lad, only nerves. It seems as if my entire life has been leading to this point. To this crowning achievement. All my studies, all my writing. All my sacrifices. Can you understand, Matthew? *Everything*."

Matthew didn't answer for a moment. He did understand a little of what the doctor was feeling. He still couldn't justify the man's obsession, but he could begin to understand. "I hope you'll be very happy together, sir."

Cornwall pulled out a handkerchief and dabbed at his eyes. "Thank you, lad. I just want you to know that I couldn't have done it without you. Our partnership has been one of the great satisfactions, indeed, one of the joys of my life." He dabbed again. "Haul away."

Matthew tugged at his system of ropes and pulleys. Nothing happened. Then he spread his legs for balance, got a really strong grip, and put all his strength into it. He pulled until sweat poured from his entire body. He pulled until his very veins stood out. Nothing happened. He loosened his grasp and stood back to study his rigging. "In the best of all possible worlds, pulleys should pull smoothly. I shouldn't need to be struggling like this," he mumbled.

"What's happening?" Cornwall fretted. "What's the problem?"

"Just a very slight delay, sir." Matthew untangled a few ropes and tried again. "Aha!" The pulleys were pulling. Smooth as silk.

"It's moving!" Cornwall cried. "More, lad. More!"

Matthew pulled more.

"That's it! That's it!"

The lid rose an inch. Two inches. The marble ball was holding the weight. Matthew hung on to his ropes, staring in fascination. Until the rope began to slip. "Push it, sir! To one side. Now!"

Cornwall woke from his own trance to shove at the lid. It swung suspended from the ropes for a breathless instant, then crashed down. Matthew secured the ropes. "Is it open? Can you see inside?"

"You look, Matthew." The doctor hovered before the breach, wringing his hands. "I haven't the strength."

Matthew trotted over to the tomb. There was a gap at one end, perhaps a foot and a half wide. He moved his head closer and was nearly overcome by the air which flowed out. Not dank like a real grave. This was different—a kind of airless air. Dead.

He shifted away. "I'll need the lamp."

Cornwall shoved it in his face. "What do you see, lad? What do you see?"

Matthew blinked at the brightness, held his breath, then bent into the tomb a second time. When his eyes adjusted, what he finally saw was unbelievable. He tried to speak, but only a croak came from his throat.

"What is it? What is it!" The doctor shoved him aside. He stuck in his own head.

"Nooooo . . ."

His wail echoed and reechoed through the tomb, through the alcove.

"Empty! No! It can't be *empty!* Where is my Voltaire? I want Voltaire! But wait—" He ducked his head back inside and emerged with a thick sheet of yellowed paper. Matthew snatched it from him.

"What have you found, sir?" He held it to the light. "It's some kind of official-looking statement, but the writing is in a funny script. Can you read it?"

Clutching his stomach, Cornwall came closer. He peered over Matthew's shoulder. "It says . . . it says. . . . 'In this year of Our Lord 1814, we, the

Ultras, have taken the remains of the ungodly devil Voltaire. We have deposited the bones where they deserve to remain for all eternity—upon a RUBBISH HEAP.'"

Cornwall crushed the sheet to his heart as the sound of midnight chimes penetrated into the depths of the crypt. Then he crumpled to the floor and wept.

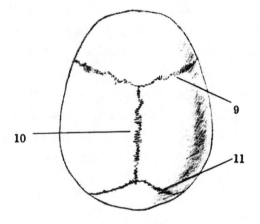

Superior aspect

CHAPTER SIXTEEN

"SIR? SIR."

The chimes heralding the New Year had long since evaporated into the night, but Asa B. Cornwall was still nursing his broken heart. Matthew racked his brains for something that might comfort his friend. Staring into the dark shadows that surrounded them in the crypt, he came up with one word. Now he swallowed his distaste, gathered his courage, and spoke it.

"*Rousseau.*"

192

Cornwall snuffled and stiffened his back against Voltaire's cold, empty tomb. "Rousseau? Jean Jacques Rousseau?"

Matthew nodded. "Didn't you say he was a famous philosopher, too?"

"'Man is born free; and everywhere he is in chains,'" the doctor intoned. "From his *Social Contract*, the bible of the French Revolution."

"So he *was* a philosopher!"

"And an educational theorist, and the man who inspired Romanticism, and the inventor of the slogan 'Liberty, Equality, Fraternity.'"

"Well, then." Matthew smiled.

"Well, what?" grumped Cornwall. "He was also a very nasty human being. Consigned all five of his children to an orphanage when he could have supported them quite easily." The doctor shook his head. "He went insane in the end, too."

"Even better," Matthew offered.

Cornwall shoved himself up another few inches. "What are you getting at, boy?"

Matthew pointed into the shadows. "There, just across the corridor. Rousseau is waiting. He should make quite an interesting study, and we've all the time in the world till morning, haven't we?"

Cornwall reached for the open ledge of

Voltaire's sarcophagus to hoist himself upright. He dusted off his trousers and straightened his jacket; pulled out his handkerchief and blew his nose with gusto. "Why are you lolling around, lad? We've got to tidy up Voltaire's tomb before we take on our new challenge. Morning isn't that far off!"

Matthew grinned and reached for the rigging.

Dr. Cornwall's consolation prize soon joined the row of skulls parading across the mantelpiece of their hotel sitting room. Matthew studied them as he warmed his hands by the fire. Rousseau had ended up to one side and a little off balance, a tad uneven with the equal spacing of Henry Bedlow, Aaron Burr, and Nicholas Mordecai. It was almost as if the three Americans were doubtful about their association with the scandalous Frenchman. Matthew decided to keep Rousseau where he was.

"Did you notice number eleven, Approbativeness, lad?" Cornwall wandered to the fire to catch Matthew contemplating Rousseau. "Never seen such a bulge. Our Frenchman lived on praise. He desired fame and glory above all." The doctor poked his finger at another spot on Rousseau's skull. "And see here, the organ of

Adhesiveness is practically recessive. Jean Jacques had definite problems with normal human attachments. I'm quite sure there was little warmth about the fellow."

Matthew stepped closer to the fire. "There's little warmth in our rooms or Paris, either, at the moment."

Cornwall was draped in a blanket wrapped around three different jackets. "Yes, winter does seem to have settled in with a vengeance." He wandered to the window and stared out over the roofs to the frozen Seine. "It's too cold to think about what to do next. It's really too cold even to write. My ink keeps freezing in its well."

He moved on to the next window, the one facing south. "It must be warmer somewhere on this blasted continent."

Matthew joined him at the window. "It's my understanding, sir, that the farther south one travels, the warmer the climate becomes. What if we were to pack our things and travel south? There's nothing keeping us in Paris any longer since—" He halted awkwardly. A full week into the New Year of 1840 and Matthew was still loath to speak the name of Voltaire aloud.

"Since my dreams were burst, lad? That's all right, you can say it." Cornwall huddled more deeply within his coverings. "The problem is, with the pinnacle of my life over and done with, nothing except Rousseau to show for it—" He hesitated before stating the obvious. "I'm feeling a little listless. . . . In point of fact, quite directionless. Here we are with a heaping war chest, and there's nothing I want to do. There's nobody I *desire*, Matthew. No one I want to acquire!"

Matthew shivered, not from the cold, but from the very plaintiveness of the man's lament. The doctor had perked up briefly during and after their acquisition of Rousseau, but for the past several days he'd been falling further and further into himself—and looking older every minute. Matthew was scared. How could he go on if something terrible happened to Dr. Cornwall? How could he pull the man from *his* slough of despond? He'd have to do something to snap his friend out of his slump. And he'd have to do it quickly.

Matthew stomped the floor and clapped his hands. Gin bounded over, expecting a walk. Matthew gave him a hug instead, then rolled onto the rug for a little wrestling match. Poor Gin had been ignored of late, too. He needed a holiday from hotel life, from city life. Matthew broke from the dog's clutch and sat up, suddenly alert.

"About the south, sir? We need a holiday. All

of us. A little time to clear our heads before we move forward."

"Move forward to *what*? I ask you, *what*?" Then Matthew's suggestion registered. "A holiday?" The very concept seemed to bemuse Cornwall further.

"Absolutely, sir. And in good time *what* we need to move forward to will present itself."

"It will?" The doctor halfheartedly waved his arms beneath their drapings. "Where might all this occur?"

"South, like I've been saying. Absolutely due south. As far as it takes to find the sun, and some heat." Matthew answered with more assurance than he felt. But someone had to take charge. "I'll go make arrangements with the concierge for a carriage and driver. If you start the packing we can leave in the morning."

Cornwall blinked. "Do you really think—"

But Matthew was already gone, Gin at his heels.

It was glorious to be on the road again. Matthew never gave the city of Paris a final glance as their carriage tumbled over the frozen, rutted highway that led south. He felt liberated. Set free of crypts and cemeteries. Delivered from the body snatcher. He'd made the right decision.

Slowly they journeyed through the Loire Valley, through the Midi, into Provence. Along the way, Matthew turned thirteen. The event came and went without remark. He was grateful merely to have survived to that milestone.

And then there came the sun, suggestions of warmth, the sea. They arrived at Cap d'Antibes and found a little pensione on the Riviera overlooking the Mediterranean Sea. At first it was just a chilly, low spit of olive-gray land. Slowly, as the doctor healed, he and Matthew began noticing more. To the north was a range of snow-covered Alps, to the south and all around was the Mediterranean, sky blue even in winter. Matthew and Gin roamed the little promontories jutting at angles into the sea. They raced around miniature bays, struggled over worn rocks, hunted for treasures to pull from the grasp of dashing waves. Cornwall sat among orange and fig trees, gazing up at palms. He sipped coffee and began making notes again. The land warmed itself into spring.

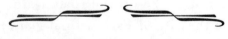

"Matthew! Matthew Morrissey!"
Matthew caught Cornwall's voice over the lull

of waves breaking by his feet. He called for Gin.
"Something must be happening, fellow. The
doctor is excited at last!" He grabbed his boots
and headed up the beach.

"What is it?"

"Fate, lad, fate!" Cornwall waved the local
newspaper in Matthew's face. "Wait till you see
what it says! *What*—not to mention *who*—has
finally presented itself!"

Matthew rolled down his trousers and pulled
on socks and boots. "Are you going to show me,
or just keep waving the news about?"

The paper was shoved under his nose.
"There." Cornwall's fingers jabbed nearly
through the page. "Read that!"

"This piece about King Louis Philippe's latest
proclamation?"

"Yes, yes! The man is trying to compensate for
the utter bourgeois drabness of his regime."

"So?" Matthew skimmed through the French
text. "So he's going to bring back Napoleon? At
least his body—"

"He's sending an expedition to the island of
St. Helena, lad. To exhume the remains of the
glorious Napoleon, buried lo these many years—
nineteen, in point of fact—and to return these
remains for proper burial in Paris, along the

199

Seine, where Napoleon always wished to be buried."

"So?" Matthew repeated.

Cornwall nearly spluttered with exasperation. "We've obviously overextended our holiday, boy. I've let you off without lessons for months. Your brain has grown dull from disuse. Think. *Think* what this means!"

Matthew was torn between elation at the doctor's reawakening and dread of the new project. He bent over Gin's sea-damp fur to hide his conflict. Of course he knew what this meant. He straightened up. "Napoleon was always the impossible goal. You never even considered him—"

"Until there was reason to consider him, lad." Cornwall chortled with glee. He was back in his element. "If one is searching for the turning points in history, what better ultimate pivotal figure to study than Napoleon Bonaparte? He changed the face of modern Europe through his wars. He even changed the face of America through the Louisiana Purchase, which helped to pay for those wars."

Asa B. Cornwall was off and running again.

"The very history of the world has always hinged on critical leaders with vision and charisma. My whole thesis hinges upon studying such men for the ultimate perfection of mankind. Such studies may make it possible to locate future originals, future superior men, super men—"

"Supermen?" Matthew broke in.

"Why not? Phrenology can identify this spark, lad. After my book reveals the critical attributes, the study of phrenology will be able to identify the next Washington, the next Jefferson—"

"The next Napoleon?" Matthew wasn't sure if that idea was good or bad. But Cornwall had no trouble with it.

"Exactly! Enough of the sea. Enough of the south. We're heading back to Paris immediately!"

"But why—"

"Because we have to worm our way onto this expedition, Matthew. The British have held an embargo on the island since Napoleon was first banished to it. There's been no way in until now. We have to get to St. Helena and exhume Napoleon before anyone else gets there first." The doctor's stubby little figure took on heroic proportions as he gazed into the horizon. "Oh yes, it will be my masterpiece. The skull of the Emperor Napoleon to study—to complete my work!"

Matthew groaned. This was far worse than

Voltaire. The entire project sounded beyond impossible. It was unimaginable. Still . . . if it made the doctor happy, if it gave him something to live for again, it was better than this half-life they'd been leading. Matthew turned to stare across the Mediterranean Sea toward whatever was beyond. He didn't even know where St. Helena was. Undoubtedly he'd find out.

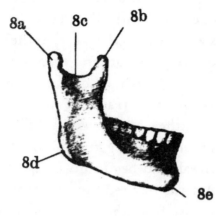

8a   8c   8b

8d

8e

CHAPTER SEVENTEEN

S⸌T. HELENA. THE ISLAND AT THE END OF THE world. The place of ultimate exile. The Emperor Napoleon's last empire. Matthew now knew where it was: a three-month sea voyage through nothing, to nowhere.

The expedition had set out from France in July on two boats, *La Favorite* and *La Belle Poule*, the command ship. This was the ship that carried the empty coffin of polished ebony emblazoned with a gold star and the name NAPOLEON. This was the ship that had its own mortuary chapel hung with black velvet covered with silver tassels and golden stars. This was the ship that carried the last living retainers of the emperor, and even the Prince de Joinville, a son of King Louis Philippe. It was also the ship that transported Dr. Asa B. Cornwall, Matthew Morrissey, and Gin.

It hadn't been easy getting aboard. Back in Paris, Cornwall had begun his campaign by having elegant cards printed, announcing his name and his avocation as the preeminent American authority on Napoleon Bonaparte. These he had sent to nearly everyone of note in the French government, along with discreet bribes. Soon Paris was buzzing with the name *Dr. ABC.* Who was this fabulously wealthy, eccentric American? A private audience with Louis Philippe himself, during which Matthew assisted at a confidential phrenological reading of the king, finally won them their wish. The war chest had become significantly lighter, but Dr. Cornwall and Associates were added to the expedition's guest list.

Now Matthew clung to the railing of *La Belle Poule* with both hands, Gin braced by his side. They both ignored the icy spray drenching them as the jagged cliffs of St. Helena appeared before them.

"There it is, my Xanadu. At last."

"What?" Matthew spun to find Dr. Cornwall beside him.

" 'Beware! Beware!' " the doctor chanted.

"*'His flashing eyes, his floating hair!*
Weave a circle round him thrice,
And close your eyes with holy dread,
For he on honey-dew hath fed,
And drunk the milk of Paradise.' "

Matthew stared at his friend. The journey had not been kind to him. Prolonged seasickness had left the doctor bereft of his comfortable pouches and paunches. He stood there like some wraith, wisps of hair blowing about burning eyes. "Have you been drinking something, sir?"

Cornwall shook his head and reason returned to his countenance. "Merely quoting Samuel Taylor Coleridge. An opium dream seemed suitable to the occasion." He glanced at the island again.

"From the books and maps I've been studying, St. Helena is ten and a half miles long, and six miles wide, situated just south of the equator in the direct line of the southeast trade winds. It's what's left of a volcano, and once—back in the sixteenth century—was considered an earthly paradise."

Earthly paradise? Matthew studied the forbidding cliffs. "It hardly seems—"

"That was before the predations of man, Matthew. It remains to be seen by our own eyes, but I believe the island has been stripped of nearly anything of worth. Save one thing."

Their ship closed in on the land. Cornwall sighed. "But our quest was never for an earthly paradise, was it? We'll know what's left soon enough." His eyes moved past the mists and deadly rocks directly ahead. "We're tacking. It looks as if we'll approach the harbor from Sandy Bay. After we pass around George Island, we ought to sight Jamestown at last. We should be disembarked before evening, lad."

A grand welcome awaited their party at the quay. There was the British governor of St. Helena, and horses and carriages; uniformed guards and liveried servants—not to mention crowds of curious onlookers from all over the island. Matthew and the doctor waited behind the important dignitaries. When their turn came, they were taken to the castle for banqueting and entertainments.

Matthew sat at one of the long tables. He ate, cautiously tossed tidbits to Gin sprawled beneath the tablecloths by his feet, and waited for something useful to come of the long speeches droning on in English and French. He would have missed it when it came if Cornwall hadn't poked him.

"Hear that, lad?"

Matthew rubbed at his drooping eyelids. "I'm not sure—"

"October fifteenth! They're raising him on October fifteenth—exactly twenty-five years to the day since Napoleon first laid eyes on St. Helena. That leaves us but eight days—"

"Hush, sir." Matthew didn't like the looks of the heads that were turning in their direction. He pasted on a bright, vacant smile. "We'll discuss it later," he whispered. "In our rooms." Then he rubbed his eyes again and added, "after we get a decent night's sleep on dry land."

When Matthew and the doctor finally awoke in the morning they wasted no time on further discussions of their goal. Instead, they set out to test their land legs and saw Jamestown in full daylight. It was not much more than a single main street of brightly whitewashed houses.

When they explored the few shops, even Cornwall shook his head in amazement at the exorbitant prices. Gin trotting beside them, the two continued their walk uphill, nonchalantly heading in the direction of Longwood, the small estate where Napoleon had lived. It was warm and humid, and soon Matthew was stripping off his jacket.

"There's not much here to justify a three-month journey, sir."

"Wait." Cornwall ignored the barren, chalky landscape surrounding them. "Rather than walking beside bare cliffs, just imagine you're strolling through a jungle of lemon trees and wild peacocks, the way it once was. We mustn't let this desolation make us forget our mission. It is to remove Napoleon from hence to a greater future."

"The French are already planning to do that, sir," Matthew observed.

"They can't give him what I can give him, lad."

Matthew kept looking around, and his doubts grew. They grew further as they walked the miles inland and finally arrived at Longwood to see the moldering, empty house with its abandoned gardens where the emperor had spent the last six years of his life. The complete futility of their mission finally hit Matthew when he spied the tomb. He stopped cold.

"There are soldiers on guard, sir!"

Cornwall rubbed at his chin. "So it would appear."

To complicate the affair, the wind rose and it began to rain.

It rained for the next week: a relentless rain, a cold and clammy rain, despite St. Helena's proximity to the equator. And the winds atop the island gusted like a small hurricane. Matthew and the doctor had been keeping a daily watch over the grave—along with the soldiers and the official caretakers. They observed the increasing desolation surrounding the tomb. The two remaining willow trees were removed and carted down-island to Jamestown to be chopped into splinters and distributed to the French sailors as souvenirs. The very patches of forget-me-nots surrounding the emperor were uprooted as keepsakes by the more sensitive French nobility. Tents were erected near the tomb. Excavations began. It was the afternoon of October fourteenth. In the morning Napoleon would be hauled from the earth.

"It's no good, sir," Matthew finally admitted. "We don't stand a chance of getting near him. You heard the soldiers talking. Napoleon lies under more than just six feet of heavy clay. Next there's a layer of cement. Ten inches beneath the cement there's a layer of stone clamped together with iron strips. Underneath all that, Napoleon is entombed inside two separate coffins." By this point in his life, Matthew had developed a certain amount of expertise on the subject of burials. He knew they were up against hopeless odds. He'd been bowed against the wind, but now struggled upright. The driving rain blurred his vision. "Somebody was really scared the emperor would get out."

"Ah, yes. The entire world was scared at that point," the doctor admitted, curiously unruffled by either the weather or the challenge. "Still, there has to be a way—"

"It will have to be after he's dug up, then," Matthew insisted. "Not before."

"Let me think on it, lad. Let me think on it. We'll come back tonight anyway, to keep vigil."

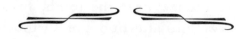

Gin had been enjoying their miles of walking each day, happy at once more being on solid ground. But even Gin was loath to leave the comfort of Matthew's cubbyhole of a castle room for more wind and rain that night.

"Come on, fellow," Matthew begged him as he attached leash to collar. "I'm not crazy about the idea, either, but we've got to do it for the doctor."

Gin whined and followed.

The walk seemed longer than ever, particularly the stretch before turning inland, the stretch that topped sheer cliffs that dropped dizzyingly into the sea. In the starless black of midnight the three pushed against the unrelenting wind and rain. Matthew paused to catch his breath and glance down those cliffs to the violence of the sea below. He wished he hadn't.

"One misstep, Gin," he murmured to the dog as he leashed him from the rim, "one misstep and we'd all be goners."

Gin yipped in agreement, then sank on his haunches to sniff the air. In a split second, the animal sprang up again. Fur bristling, he flung back his head and let out a deep-throated bay the likes of which Matthew had heard only once before. And that time it had been on the brink of his consciousness, on the edges of a long tunnel . . .

"Doctor! Sir!"

Cornwall was already frozen a few steps ahead. "It's impossible! Gin has only ever reacted that way to—"

A shape emerged from the rocks surrounding them. It was dark as the night, wrapped tightly in a cape, with a hat pulled low to conceal its face. Instinctively, Matthew rubbed at the raised scar on his cheek.

"Run, sir! For your life! It's the body snatcher!"

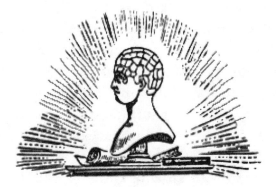

CHAPTER EIGHTEEN

SUDDENLY HE WAS BEFORE THEM, HIS FORM SEEMING
to encompass and swallow the entire night sky. As
the wind snatched off his hat and whipped his
cape wide, the open cloak revealed a hand brandishing his weapon of choice—a long knife.

Gin let out a second harrowing bay and
crouched for attack. That was when Matthew discovered his fingers were caught in the dog's leash.

The body snatcher laughed. It was a sound even
more frightening than his fearful demeanor.

"Chickenhearted cowards! Hiding behind a dog. It won't save you this time. Nothing will. Thought you could keep me in jail, didn't you. No jail can hold me!" He laughed again. "Now I'll have what I've been after for so long!"

"But, but—" Matthew was madly trying to untangle himself while Gin strained against his collar to the point of suffocation. "How did you find us this time? How did you get to St. Helena?"

"Fool! Your names were all over Paris—and an able seaman with an able knife"—he flashed the blade pointedly—"can always carve out a job for himself."

"You were on the second ship." Cornwall hadn't run after all. Now he actually took a step closer, swinging his ever-present satchel. "*La Favorite.* After all this time and effort, perhaps you'd be kind enough to reveal what you're after, what it is you've been seeking from us."

"*Re-veal what I've been seeking?* Mutton-headed swell." The body snatcher spat. "I'll *re-veal* right enough, and have my revenge, too. Revenge for all those months in that hideous hellhole you sent me to. Swallowing nothing but bread and water and rat made me more than hunger for escape. It made me hungry for *final* solutions."

He brandished the knife again and the dreadful laughter returned. This time it changed into a shriek as Matthew finally freed himself.

Gin leaped straight for the body snatcher. The dog went for the knife arm first, and the weapon slipped from the villain's grasp to clang onto the rocks. As he backed off in sudden fear, Gin sprang again. This time they wrestled. It was wrestling far different from the play between Matthew and Gin. Man and dog rolled over and over, both biting, scratching, gouging. Closer and closer to the cliff's edge they rolled, a tangle of fur and cape and leash. Their snarls joined into one inhuman din.

"Call off your cur!" the body snatcher screeched at last. "I'll tell you . . . all!"

Matthew tried, but Gin wouldn't be called off. His jaws found the man's leg, his teeth sank deeply into flesh and bone. The body snatcher howled and jerked with agony until his head was over the brink, hanging on thin air.

"Tombe!" he yelped.

"Whose tomb?" Cornwall yelled.

"Nobody's . . ." His shoulders had followed his head over the edge, and the body snatcher was thrashing wildly with his arms. Trying desperately to grab something solid. Trying desperately to save his life.

It was enough for Matthew.

"Stop, Gin! Heel!"

He dove into the melee to wrest Gin free. He caught the dog's rear legs and pulled with all his might. The leash freed itself to slap him smartly in the face.

"He wanted your papers," the body snatcher gasped. "Charles . . ."

Gin loosened his jaws for a split second. His victim jerked away with relief—in the wrong direction.

"Toooooooombe . . ."

Over the cliff the body snatcher tumbled, plunging into the abyss of night and sea. Matthew fell back inches from the same fate, hanging on to Gin for dear life. When the dog's quivering slowed, he ventured a final look over the cliff's edge. It was too dark. He could see nothing but the whitecapped spume of waves pounding against rock. He finally turned. The doctor was sitting bolt upright on the closest rock.

"Well. Imagine that." He smiled and tapped the satchel in his lap. "My manuscript has been authenticated at last, lad. If the great Charles Tombe wants it that badly, it's legitimate!"

"Tombe. Your scholar and gentleman. It's

been *him* behind the body snatcher all this time? Not the Fowlers? Not some mysterious conspiracy?" Matthew sat rocking Gin, calming the dog, calming himself. He found his voice again. "Your manuscript is now legitimate. That's all you can say about this entire affair? About a man's death?"

"Tut, tut. The body snatcher received his just reward at long last. It was either him or us, after all."

"True, but watching someone actually *die*—" Is that what he'd wanted all along for the fiend who'd been pursing them? For the hideous man who'd left him scarred for life? Was he that bloodthirsty in his heart of hearts? Had he desired revenge as wickedly as the body snatcher? Matthew shivered, once more unsure of many things. Unsure even of the doctor, who'd watched—only watched—as the whole incident unfolded.

"He was still a *man*, sir. A living human being. Not one of your dried-out skulls." Matthew breathed deeply a few times, working things out in his mind. Maybe he'd had enough of the entire game. Maybe it was time to end it.

"Gin and I are walking back, Doctor. We'll take a carriage tomorrow with the other functionaries. We'll watch Napoleon Bonaparte being exhumed in *dignity.* You may join us or not, as you choose."

Matthew rose and began retracing his steps down the steep path, Gin panting wearily at his heels. Tightly clutching his precious satchel, Asa B. Cornwall eventually followed, a beatific smile on his face.

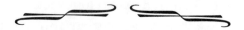

Another tent had been raised. This one was directly next to Napoleon's tomb itself. Matthew stood sheltered among the gathering listening to the deluge overhead, watching the coffin rise, sluiced with rain. In hushed silence it was borne into the tent and set within the waiting sarcophagus. The lid of the first coffin was forced open. Within lay the second coffin. That was forced, too. A priest sprinkled holy water and prayed, "'Out of the depths I have cried unto thee, O Lord.'" Then the second lid was raised.

A gasp burst through the crowd.

Matthew inched closer, trying to catch the low buzz of voices, trying to see. And then he saw. He gasped himself. There were no bones. There was no neat, clean skull.

Napoleon Bonaparte was a mummy! A perfectly preserved mummy!

His jacket was still green, with a red lining. The medals and buttons decorating the uniform were tarnished, but his face—his face! It was pale, with a stubble of new beard growing on his cheeks.

"He looks," Matthew whispered, "he looks so young, and almost alive!"

"So strong," murmured one old servant.

"So virile," muttered another.

"Vive Napoléon!" a general cried out.

His shout was taken up by others among the French.

"Vive Napoléon! Vive Napoléon!"

The British soldiers began to look wary. As they adjusted the rifles on their shoulders, Dr. Cornwall tapped at Matthew's.

"It might be politic to disappear at this point, lad. Before the second Revolution begins."

There was silence in their carriage for half the journey down the precipitous track and back to Jamestown. There had, in fact, been silence between Matthew and the doctor since the attack on the cliff the night before. Cornwall still hung on to his satchel, but now he glanced from it to Matthew and back again. At last he cleared his throat.

"Perhaps I was a little heartless last night, lad."
He waited. When nothing was returned, he tried
again. "But surely you understand my feelings at
the time—"

"You didn't come to our rescue, sir." Matthew
finally spit out what had become his foremost
concern. "My nightmare stood before me, and
you didn't even try to help Gin and me. You just
stood there."

"What was I supposed to use for a weapon? I
had no stick, and Gin seemed to be thoroughly
on top of the situation." He chuckled.

"Not funny," Matthew managed. "You had
your satchel. You could have hit him with your
satchel."

"Accost the body snatcher with my satchel?
Risk having my life's work—nay, my very *life*—
swept over the cliff? Gone forever?" He hugged
the bag to his chest in fear and trembling at the
thought.

Matthew scowled. "If that's how you still feel
about it, don't you think it's time to get your
precious manuscript published at last? So this
same thing doesn't happen again?" He paused.
"Or are you afraid to get it published?"

Cornwall turned white and shrank farther away
from Matthew. Beads of sweat appeared in a thin

line across his brow. His death grip on the satchel intensified. "Of course I've been afraid to get it published! Afraid of the scorn that might rain down on my head from the scholarly world." His tense fingers loosed a little as he added most humbly, "I'm a coward at heart, Matthew, don't you see?"

"Give it up, sir. Face your demons, the way I faced mine. Publish."

"Face my demons . . ." Cornwall whispered. He dropped the bag at last. "Maybe it is time to let go of Mrs. Carey's chickens, to let go of my past." He swiped at his forehead. "I'll do it! Now that I no longer have to live in fear." He stopped. "Except for one thing."

Matthew turned toward the doctor. "What are you scared of now?"

"I'm scared, lad, that you might leave me. That you and your great beast—having discovered me for the worthless scoundrel I am—might walk out of my life as randomly as you walked into it." He pushed the satchel from his lap to the side of his seat. "It suddenly occurs to me that losing your companionship would be far worse than losing my manuscript."

Matthew's head spun until he could hold in his thoughts no longer.

"You're not a worthless scoundrel! You never were. How could a worthless scoundrel have fed me, and taught me French, and philosophy, and mathematics—and the science of phrenology?"

Cornwall heaved out a great sigh. "Then I'm forgiven? I swear, lad. First things first in future. You and Gin. As for the manuscript, we'll find a publisher in Paris and get the albatross off my back—"

"What about completing Part Two?" Matthew asked. "How can you get it published without Part Two?"

"You do care!" Cornwall beamed. "As for the completion, I believe I've finally conquered my *mal de mer*. And a long voyage without seasickness leaves any number of hours for writing—not to mention *research*."

By this point in their relationship, Matthew knew Cornwall's code words as well as he knew the old rascal himself. He picked right up on this one, as if there'd never been a bone of contention between himself and his master. "There'll be a guard on Napoleon all the way back to France, sir. Day and night. He'll be guarded until the moment he's set in his new resting place."

"Les Invalides," Cornwall murmured. "With all the other old soldiers. Yes, you're right, of course.

But it's not a simple skull we're dealing with any-more, is it?" He hummed softly to himself, happily enmeshed once more in his plots. "And soldiers can be bribed even more efficiently than aristocrats. *N'est-ce pas?*"

Matthew squirmed uncomfortably on his hard seat. There was one final point of contention after all. "But you can't just behead him—not with him . . . like that!"

"I have no intentions of beheading an emperor, Matthew." Cornwall's eyes twinkled. "But three months at sea is quite a long time, quite a long time to do a complete phrenological study of a perfectly preserved head."

"You'll just study his head? He won't join our collection?"

"By that time we will possess the information. And as much as one might desire the souvenir . . ." The doctor sighed. "Alas, sometimes one must relinquish the artifact for the greater good. In this case, for the greater good of France. *La Belle France.* She's really been quite decent to us."

Matthew felt relief course through his body. "And then what, sir?"

"And then what?" Cornwall chuckled. "And then we move forward, lad, onward and upward. There are other books to be written, and our war chest is still amazingly healthy. We must continue to think big. Think of Charlemagne . . . think of Julius Caesar . . . think of—"

"Alexander the Great?" Matthew offered, back in the game again.

"That's the spirit, lad!" Asa B. Cornwall fondly patted Matthew's arm, then bent to caress Gin at his feet. "Think *epic*."

Author's Note

THE NINETEENTH CENTURY WAS ALIVE WITH intellectual possibilities opened up by the success of the Industrial Revolution, Romanticism, and Darwin's theory of evolution. Ideas literally swarmed between Europe and the New World—some of them more rational than others. Phrenology was one of these ideas.

Phrenology was conceived by the German physician Franz Joseph Gall (1758–1828) around 1800 as a theory of brain structure. It was his idea that talents and other qualities could be traced to the functions of particular areas of the brain, and the shape of the skull. Gall's student Johann Kaspar Spurzheim (1776–1832) coined the term phrenology, meaning "science of the mind," and became world-famous in the course of promoting this study. Spurzheim lectured on the Continent and in Great Britain, dissecting brains and picking up followers, such as the lawyer George Combe (who, with my apologies, became the inspiration for Charles Tombe). During a lecture tour of America in 1832, Spurzheim's health broke and he died in Boston. Spurzheim's brain, which weighed a mighty fifty-seven ounces, was preserved as a medical memento.

Meanwhile, two young Amherst College students, Henry Beecher Ward and Orson Squire Fowler, were following the phrenology lectures in Boston and became entranced with the subject. Fowler made it his lifetime profession, opening (with his brother Lorenzo) a phrenological emporium in New York City in the mid-1830s. Fowler turned phrenology into a practical—and very American—phenomenon. By the late 1830s, hundreds of books and pamphlets on phrenology had been published. Americans were wild to have the bumps on their heads read, wild to be told what their possibilities could be, based on their phrenological analyses. They wanted to be told how to choose a profession, how to select a wife, how to be happy—and practical phrenologists were willing to do the telling for a fee.

Phrenology reached its peak in the 1860s, then slowly degenerated into a carnival sideshow. During its heyday, though, it had a tremendous influence on thought in the United States. As a scientific study, it is sometimes considered a precursor to Sigmund Freud and psychoanalysis.

So, phrenological charts and busts were produced in large quantities, and phrenology was considered a serious system of thought. The Fowler brothers were real, and quite harmless. What about the body snatcher?

Body snatchers, or resurrectionists, were a part of New York City's underworld from the late eighteenth century into the mid—nineteenth century. They existed because they filled a need. It was illegal to dissect bodies, yet medical students desperately needed bodies in order to learn their profession. Body snatchers prowled cemeteries, waiting for fresh burials to supply the market. Outraged editorials were written in the newspapers. Watchmen were hired to protect the newly buried—and just as quickly bribed to turn their backs. It was not until 1854 that the Bone Bill, an "Act to Promote Medical Science," made dissection legal in the state of New York by giving medical schools access to unclaimed bodies. Body snatchers were permanently out of work.

Napoleon Bonaparte *was* exhumed on St. Helena in 1840 and returned in glory to France, his head intact. Voltaire's tomb in the Pantheon *was* desecrated by radicals and left empty. As for Dr. Asa B. Corwall and Matthew Morrissey, they are strictly figments of my imagination. But I firmly believe that science and mutual affection led them forward in quest of Alexander the Great!

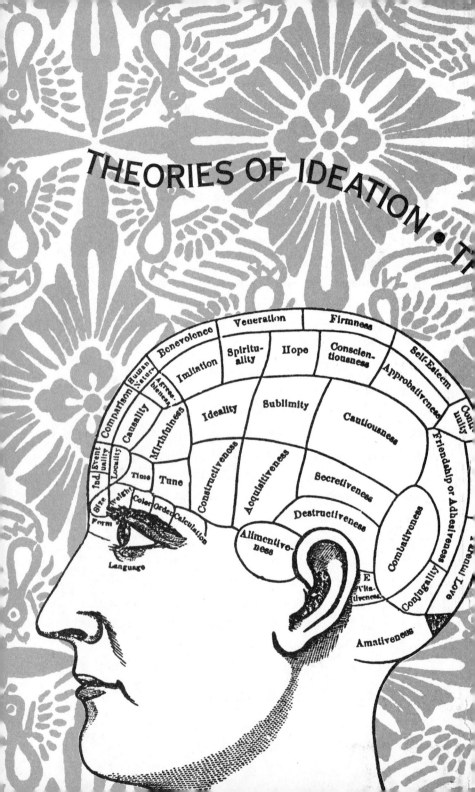

THEORIES OF IDEATION · TH